COURT OF NIGHT

CRAWFORD C.N.

c.n. crawford

Copyright © 2018 by Crawford C.N.

All rights reserved.

No part of this book may be reproduced in any form or by any electronic or mechanical means, including information storage and retrieval systems, without written permission from the author, except for the use of brief quotations in a book review.

CHAPTER 1

I stared at the gruesome offering, bile rising in my throat. Someone had nailed a human arm to one of the exterior doors of the Institute—driven the spike right through the palm, onto the wooden door.

It smelled like a fresh kill. Sticky blood oozed down the severed elbow, dripping onto the pavement. Frowning at it, I clutched the straps of my bug-out bag. Touching severed body parts wasn't my favorite way to spend the day.

And yet I had to move the thing, because behind the hand, a blank piece of paper hung on the door. A note, probably? Given the method of delivery, I could only assume it was important, and probably not something nice like a thank-you card.

Grimacing, I pulled at the nail. My stomach churned at the faint slithering sound it made, my hand brushing against the cold flesh. Thick blood coated the tips of my fingers. When I had pulled the nail all the way out, the arm fell to the pavement with a wet *thud*.

I snatched the paper and flipped it over, finding a letter scrawled in blood.

As I read its contents, my pulse pounded in my ears.

Arianna,

Tomorrow night, deliver Ruadan to me. He should wait for me outside the Institute's gate, unarmed and wearing iron cuffs. Fail, and London will suffer the Great Mortality once more. In case you think I don't possess that power, I've already started with a small population on the Isle of Dogs.

I'll wait till nine at night tomorrow, then everyone dies.

And Arianna, my darling. If you fail me, I'll let everyone know what you really are. How long will you survive, then?

Love,

Baleros

My stomach dropped, and my hands were shaking so hard I could barely rip the note into pieces.

No one could see this letter. No one.

Frantically, I tore bits off the paper. One piece after another, I shredded it.

I'll let everyone know what you really are.

Fear had gripped my throat. What if someone glued the scraps back together? I shifted my bug-out bag off my shoulders and rummaged around until I found a lighter.

Should have started with the burning.

Crouching on the ground, I brushed the bits of paper into a small pile over the stone, then held a flame over them. I had a hard time igniting them, and I burnt my thumb.

It wasn't enough that he'd stolen an *entire* mist army from the Institute. It wasn't enough that he'd imprisoned Ruadan's mother, the Queen of Emain. None of that was enough power for him. He had to have everything, didn't he? He had to have it all.

Baleros's twenty-third law of power: Use terror to control your subjects.

He knew me well enough to understand what would terrify me: the truth. What if Ruadan saw this?

2

I stuck my burnt finger in my mouth, sucking on it. Then, I leaned down again toward the small pile, igniting it from the top. A tendril of smoke curled around me.

Baleros might have a flair for the dramatic, but my old gladiator master did not make idle threats. If he said he was going to kill people, he meant it. If he said he'd reveal the truth about me, he meant that, too. He wanted the World Key on Ruadan's chest, and he wouldn't stop until he got it.

Pieces of paper stuck to my blood-smudged fingers. What, exactly, was the Great Mortality? Whatever it was, it didn't sound like a wonderful time. It sounded like a lot of death.

Still, I'd give up my own arm before I handed over Ruadan in chains. Not only had I grown attached to the giant, brooding demigod, but I wasn't about to present Baleros with all the power he wanted in the form of the World Key.

I exhaled. I had only a few more pieces to ignite, now, on the cobbles. I singed my fingers again and cursed under my breath.

"What the hells are you doing?" A deep voice sent my pulse racing.

Slowly, I turned to find to find Aengus glaring down at me. As one of the Institute's most powerful Knights, his steady, green gaze sometimes unnerved me. Plus, he didn't really like me.

"What's the problem?" I tried to keep my tone light. *Nothing to see here, folks.*

"You're crouching next to a severed human arm," he said. "Burning tiny scraps of paper. I'd venture to say it's not a typical way to spend a Tuesday morning."

I rose, trying to smile. *Stick as close to the truth as possible.* "I found a note along with the arm. I didn't want it to create more panic than necessary." The panic, in this case, was my own, but Aengus didn't need to know that. "The humans in this city have been freaking out for weeks," I added. "Baleros has been terrorizing London with his army. No reason to make them panic anymore."

"What did the note say?" He wasn't letting this point go.

"It was from Baleros, of course. We have until nine tomorrow night to hand over Ruadan in chains, or Baleros unleashes the Great Mortality. And apparently he already started on the Isle of Dogs."

"Bloody hells. If that's true, we need to contain that."

"I know." I clenched my jaw. "What exactly is the Great Mortality?"

"It's the plague that killed scores of people in Europe several times over. The Black Death, some people call it. How the hells is he capable of this magic?"

I nodded. "I have no idea. But you can put 'dying of the Plague' in your agenda book for tomorrow night unless we can kill Baleros between now and then."

He narrowed his eyes. "We once had a gorta here, guarding the gate, but you killed him. Do you know how hard it is to find a good gorta?"

"Quite hard, I imagine, or we'd already have one," I replied. "Why are we talking about this right now?"

"Because we have no gorta. No guard on duty. No witnesses. You burned the letter. Now, we have only your word to go on. How convenient for you."

Ever since I'd stabbed Ruadan and run off with the Institute's lumen crystal, Aengus had been a bit frosty. Apparently, he frowned on violent assault and theft.

I crushed the ashes into the cobbles with my foot. "I don't know what planet you're coming from, but I don't think there's anything convenient about dying from the Plague, Aengus."

And with that stinging rebuke, I strode through the Institute's blood-smeared door, leaving Aengus behind with the severed arm.

* * *

Standing outside The Spread Eagle, I took a long sip of Maker's Mark. Tension gripped my body. Pigeons cooed in the bridge that arched overhead, their calls slowly drowned out by the rumbling of a train.

A reckoning was coming to the great city of London—and I had my own personal reckoning in store. Baleros was the only one in London who knew the truth about me, and he'd hold it over my head as long as he was alive. Blackmail I couldn't ignore.

It had been twelve hours since I'd found the note. During that time, Ruadan had sent out most of the knights on a mission to hunt down Baleros. He'd kept only two behind: Aengus and me.

So far, no one had reported anything useful. All we had was bad news: the plague outbreak on the Isle of Dogs had been confirmed.

As far as we could tell, Baleros had been moving from one place to another, never staying in one spot long enough to get caught. The last place we'd tracked him to was an apartment in Barbican. He'd left only a half a pack of cigarettes and a box of cereal, and the cloaked knights had zoomed off after him to the next location.

In my case, tonight, I'd left the cloak at home. I was undercover in an ordinary pair of leggings and a sweater.

Once upon a time—like, two weeks ago—the Shadow Fae were the only ones wandering around London in cloaks. I mean, who else would do weird shit like that?

But now? There were these *other* cloaked people. Cloaked people who pushed people into oncoming trains, then jumped after them. In the Institute, someone had started calling them jackdaws because of their dark gray and black cloaks, and the name stuck.

Who were they? We didn't know. But the rest of London? They had a pretty good idea. They saw cloaks, they thought *Shadow Fae.* Simple as that.

In other words, someone was framing us, and I had a strong hunch it was Baleros. Maybe—just maybe—one of these jackdaws could take us to their leader.

I touched the lumen stone around my neck. A gift of magic from Ruadan—one that would help me move around fast if I found one of these cloaked men.

From the pub windows behind me, a piercing song floated through the glass. A woman was singing karaoke—or, more accurately, screaming it. Alanis Morissette, over and over.

I frowned at her through the fogging class. *Bloody hells, woman. Just download a dating app and move on.*

Footfalls turned my head, and my heart sped up at the sight of Ruadan prowling toward me. Dark magic curled around him. The edges of his broad body seemed indistinct, like a photograph shot out of focus. But he still stood out to me, those violet eyes like a beacon in the night. Even with his fuzzy appearance, I felt acutely aware of every one of the thickly corded muscles under his dark clothes. Every movement of his called to me—the breathing, the purposeful gait —precise and focused under the fog of his magic.

As he stepped closer to me, he began to look sharper. The distant streetlights washed over his perfect face. His serene beauty belied the ruthlessness underneath. I sipped my drink.

When he reached me, he leaned against the wall. This close, his magic vibrated over my skin, making my toes curl. His magic was disturbingly addictive.

"Hello, Grand Master."

"What have you found?" No greetings, just right to the point.

"I haven't seen any of the jackdaws yet, but I will. They stick near the Institute, and they usually linger around this overpass. I'll see one soon."

"What did the note say?" Ruadan asked.

Oh. So he'd been speaking to Aengus. "I already told your mate. It said we needed to hand you over by tomorrow night, or Baleros will unleash the Great Mortality. That's the Plague."

"I know what it is. What *else* did the note say?"

I'd been hoping to skip over that part. I took another sip of the whiskey. "What makes you think it said something else?"

"You burnt it."

I was a terrible liar, so I decided to stick with a simple statement of fact. "You still don't trust me."

His dark magic stroked my skin, a subtle reminder of his overwhelming power. It had a primordial feel to it that made my spine straighten.

He took another step closer, his muscled form looming over me. "I can hear your heart race when you get nervous. And your cheeks flush."

I knew exactly how to throw Ruadan off.

I licked my lips. "How do you know that's nervousness and not lust?"

His muscles tensed.

I took one step closer, nearly touching him, and an electrical charge buzzed between our bodies. "You seem very in tune with my physiological reactions. There's something very appealing about that."

His eyes darkened. I shivered as his magic dragged the temperature down.

My jaw tightened. It didn't seem my flirting had worked to distract him. "Look, Baleros knows things about me. Things I don't want anyone else to find out. He's black-mailing me. We give you over, or he tells everyone. That's why I burnt it."

There it was—the truth. As much of it as I was willing to tell.

"What things?" His commanding tone set my teeth on edge.

Another sip of my whiskey, and I let the silence hang over us. Then, I narrowed my eyes. "Like you don't have your own secrets. You hardly speak. I'm sure there's plenty you haven't told me."

Ruadan looked away from me, his eyebrows furrowed. Then, he nodded. I was dead on with the "you have secrets, too" theory.

"Try to report back to me within an hour. If the jackdaws don't lead to anything, we'll track him another way."

Ruadan started to turn back to the Institute, but the pub door slammed open, and he froze. The heartbroken karaoke singer stumbled outside, and Ruadan turned to her. Rivulets of mascara ran down her face, and her lipstick had been smeared over her chin. She sloshed a bit of white wine out of her glass.

Ruadan stared at the drunk woman, who was singing quietly to herself. His eyes darkened, body going completely still.

I took another look at the woman. She was beautiful, sure. Big blue eyes, full lips, rosy cheeks. But apart from that, she seemed like an ordinary human—nothing remarkable or stare-worthy. She wiped a hand under her nose, then sniffled into her wineglass.

Ruadan's gaze was locked on her. A faint hint of violet

glowed off him. His magic seemed to be intensifying, pulsing in delicious waves that skimmed over my skin.

Pleasurable as it felt, it seemed he'd forgotten all about me, his eyes black as voids. Then, he closed his eyes, breathing in deeply. Was he smelling her? What the hells was going on here?

CHAPTER 2

I crossed my arms. "You were saying I needed to report back," I said, my voice unnecessarily harsh.

The black snapped out of his eyes, and he turned his violet gaze to me. The air seemed to glow around him, and the drunk woman simply swayed, staring at him like she was transfixed.

"It's just like I said," I added. "We all have our secrets, don't we?" I turned to the woman. "Can you piss off, now? It's not safe out here. Shadow Fae all over the place." Was I being a bit territorial? Perhaps.

She nodded, her eyes still on Ruadan, then pulled open the pub door again and disappeared inside.

Before I could say another word to Ruadan, darkness billowed around him, and he was gone.

I surveyed the empty street. There hadn't been many humans around in the past few weeks. Not since Baleros had begun his recent reign of terror with his own growing army.

A couple rounded the corner—middle-aged, but dressed from head to toe in piercings and leather. As they walked, I tuned into their conversation.

"Should we really be out so close to the Institute?" the woman hissed. "The Shadow Fae might murder us."

There it was again. All it had taken was a few black cloaks to confuse the entire city of London.

The man glanced over his shoulders. "Keep it down, Lucy. They could be anywhere."

My plan was simple: find one of the cloaked buggers, then hurt him until I found out more. If my hunch was right, the jackdaws were connected to Baleros. We'd find him, imprison him, demand to know where Ruadan's mother was. Then we'd kill him.

Or, at least, that's how it would all work out in my head.

But things were never that easy, were they? And why weren't there any jackdaws around here tonight? It was like they were avoiding me. Or avoiding *something*.

I sniffed the air, and a faint, earthy scent hit me. Mossy and dank—a fae smell, but an unfamiliar one. Older than most fae, and a bit more coppery. It smelled of death. I slid my glass onto the windowsill. Maybe this was what they were avoiding.

I started walking north, and as I reached an empty intersection, a blur of movement sent my pulse racing. I turned, catching a glimpse of a woman crossing toward a narrow alleyway.

There she was—the fae I'd scented. She reeked of death.

Just before she disappeared into the alleyway, she turned to look at me. Immediately, I could tell I'd been right about the fae thing—long, metallic talons; rapid, animalistic movements. When her eyes met mine, my pulse quickened. Her skin was the color of bone, and a dress hugged her body, its leather the color of dried blood. Long, black hair hung down her back, and her eyes had the blue-gray hue of a murky lake. She opened her mouth, and for just a moment, a forked tongue snaked out. Then, she pivoted, marching onward.

I wasn't sure what was happening, but this was a lead worth chasing. An ancient, powerful fae like this one wasn't an everyday occurrence.

I pulled a knife out of my bug-out bag as I walked, wishing I'd come armed with a sword instead. It's just that swords tended to ruin the whole *ordinary human* undercover vibe.

I followed her through the alley, which opened up into another street.

When I reached the mouth of the alley, the fae turned back to look at me, murky eyes landing on my face. Across the street, three men in white football shirts were chanting a song, drunkenly stumbling into each other. One of them carried a pint that sloshed on the pavement.

The fae's attention darted back to them. She wasn't interested in me.

I stared as her form began to change, her skin scaling over. A sharp, knobbled spine protruded from the back of her dress.

My pulse raced faster. The men in the football shirts hadn't even noticed her. My fingers twitched on my knife hilt as I waited to see what she'd do next.

I had my answer when her shockingly long tongue shot out, lashing the three men across their faces. The attack left deep, red gashes in their skin, and the men staggered, shouting now.

I took a step closer. I didn't want to intervene yet—I wanted to find out exactly what she was.

The men seemed to be frozen in place. From fear, perhaps? Whatever it was, it didn't look as if they could move.

The lower half of the fae's body then shifted, elongating and growing scales, becoming a tail with a rattle that then slithered across the road toward the men.

I touched the lumen stone at my neck, then narrowed my focus to a single point near the fae, willing myself to summon its magic. Electric power crackled up my spine. I got ready to leap, and—

The fae's head whipped toward me, tongue lashing out. She struck me in the neck, ripping through the skin. As soon as her tongue made contact, my muscles began to seize up, body freezing. I stood immobilized as she turned her attention to the three men again. Her tail wrapped around them like a ribbon encircling a bunch of flowers. Their eyes went wide, faces red as she squeezed their chests. Garbled grunts rose from their throats. They couldn't breathe, and with each gasp, she seemed to tighten her grip even more.

She was squeezing the poor bastards to death. I tried opening my mouth to scream, but even my mouth was frozen, and I couldn't move my vocal cords. The only sounds in this deserted street were a low hissing rising from the ancient fae and the strangled gasps coming from the men. Gripped around the waist, they made a gruesome bouquet of humans, eyes popping.

The fae's body glowed as her tail constricted further around them. Dark veins shot through the men's skin—a poison from her tongue, perhaps?

With an iron will, I forced my neck muscles to move just a little, then my eyes. I looked down at my own body, nauseated to see dark toxins pulsing through my veins. I felt as if I were rotting from the inside out. Wrath pulsed along with the poison. What *right* did she have to do this to me?

When I forced my eyes up again, two of the three men had died—suffocated in her grasp. The third, horrifyingly, was being crushed against the corpses of his friends. I opened my mouth again to scream, and this time a tiny sound emerged from my throat—a little squeak. But what good did that do me? All I could do was stare as she crushed the breath out of the last man, his face now purple.

As soon as the life left his eyes, her tail slithered away from the rotten bouquet. She transformed back into her legged form.

I stood there, frozen, like an idiot.

I understood what she was a *fomoire*, a fae who fed off suffering. A living nightmare. In fact, that's where the word came from—night-moire. If I hadn't been here, she'd probably have prolonged their suffering just to feed off it. But now she had a second target. Me, immobilized by her poison.

Her head swiveled back to me, body glowing with a pale blue light. She stalked closer, high heels clacking over the pavement. Her jerky gait reminded me of a fox walking on its hind legs, and she seemed like an animal wearing a human suit more than a fae.

I strained, desperate to grip the knife at my side, desperate to thrust it into her chest.

Three crushed humans, and me unable to move. This day was not going well for me. As she moved closer, I could see the pale, greenish tinge to her porcelain skin.

When she was just a few inches away from me, I braced, expecting her tail to come out again. To my surprise, she pulled a silver cigarette case from her pocket. She opened it and pulled out a smoke. She lit it, put it in her mouth, then offered the case to me. "Smoke?"

I could hardly say *no*, could I? I mean, I literally couldn't say anything at all.

She cocked her head, smiling. Then, she jammed a cigarette in my mouth, just between my gritted teeth. She lit it, and smoke curled into my eyes, making them water. I *hated* this woman.

"There," she trilled. "Now you look relaxed."

The cigarette fell out of my mouth, along with a thin stream of drool. Lovely evening I was having so far.

Right now, I pretty much wanted to rip her throat out with my bare hands, but the immobilization put a kink in that desire. Why wasn't she crushing me to death?

She blinked at me. "They were enjoying themselves. I had to make them suffer. You understand, don't you? You know what I am. I feed off pain." She leaned in closer, sniffing me. "But you were already suffering before I got to you."

Rage simmered. What was she talking about?

A smile curled her lips as she looked me up and down. "Guilt. Loneliness. Fear. Not of me—no. You're afraid of yourself. Afraid of people knowing the truth." She closed her eyes, breathing in. "It's lovely." When she opened her eyes again, her body was growing brighter. "It's all right, darling. I'm going to kill you, and then you don't have to worry anymore. I'm here to end your suffering."

Bitch, please.

I closed my eyes, summoning the darkness from within. Cold wrath flooded me. Yes, the snake lady was terrifying— but so was I.

CHAPTER 3

These beasts, crawling over the earth, acting like gods. She needs to learn her place.

The voice in my mind wasn't quite my own. It scared me, but I knew it would save me.

A blast of dark magic pulsed out of my body like a toxic cloud. It pounded through my blood, pushing out her poison.

Here it was—my dark side. The part of me I had to keep secret. I was the fury of the gods, and I had my own venom.

The darkness had exploded for just a few moments. Then, the magic had snapped back into me again. My body shook and nausea gripped my gut. I hunched over, vomiting up my whiskey onto the pavement.

Holy crap. Had that actually just happened? Had the real me nearly come out? Panic had such a tight grip on my mind that I nearly forgot about the fae.

I'd nearly lost control.

I looked at the ancient fae, who lay flat on her back—hurt, but still breathing. My little burst of dark magic had flattened her. More importantly, it had freed my muscles.

Fighting nausea, I twirled my knife, my sights locked on her.

I smiled. She hadn't seen this coming.

Her eyes opened wider. "What *are* you?"

Fury of the gods.

"I'm your worst nightmare." It came out in a voice I didn't recognize—many voices, in fact; a chorus of them, harmonizing with each other.

She narrowed her eyes at me, then pulled out another cigarette. With what seemed a great deal of effort, she rose to her feet.

Should I let her live?

"You and I are the same, darling," she said. "We're monsters. The only difference is that you're lying to yourself."

Nope. You don't get to live.

I lunged for her, slashing with my knife. She darted back, her movements bestial. Her tongue lashed out again, striking me in the side. Pain seared me, but her poisons didn't seep into me this time. She hit me again with her tongue, but this time, I cut into it with my blade. Dark blood stained the pavement.

Battle fury pulsed through my bones, and I lunged for her, ready to stab, to slice, to carve.

A rattle rose from her throat, and she darted away from me again, landing in a puddle of water with a splash. She was *fast*.

I lunged for her again, but she disappeared into the puddle. Her body vanished completely.

She left behind only the smell of moss and blood. I looked at the pile of human corpses, my stomach turning. It was only then I realized that my whole body was trembling, that the knife in my hand was shaking. I didn't feel in control of the death force in me, and I wanted to keep it locked up.

I let out a long, slow breath. I couldn't let my dark side come out—not completely.

I stared at the puddle of murky water, marshaling a sense of calm. One more night, and I still didn't have any answers.

I didn't know if that woman was directly connected to Baleros, but his chaos had allowed her to roam London's streets, feeding off death. I cocked my head, staring at the still puddle. Maybe now that I'd rid the streets of her death-stench, I could find myself some jackdaws.

I shoved my hands into my pockets and turned to walk back toward The Spread Eagle.

The streets still looked empty, and I attuned my ears to the sound of footsteps. Ruadan had given me a time limit on this particular mission, and I had about a half hour left before I was supposed to report back to him. I was starting to think I'd be late.

It took me another twenty minutes before I found one of them, stalking down Fenchurch Street. The oldest part of the city, where humans had once made sacrifices to the river gods.

My pulse started to race as I turned to follow him, and I sheathed my knife again. He was heading south, toward The Spread Eagle. When he turned his head, I caught a hollow look in his eyes that made my blood run cold. He didn't seem to be taking things in, didn't notice me. He was human, but the expression in his eyes made me think he was staring at me from one of the hells itself. What had Baleros done to these men?

I picked up my pace, moving after him to close the gap. I shoved my hand into my pocket, then pulled out a grape lolly to pop in my mouth.

When the jackdaw turned left into a narrow alleyway—not far from the glowing spires of the Institute—I followed him into the passage.

His footsteps echoed off the brick walls. I quickened my pace, drawing my knife as I moved closer. Then, when I was within arm's reach, I grabbed him. In the next heartbeat, I had him pinned up against the wall, elbow to his chest, knife to his throat.

That wasn't hard. Not hard at all.

He stared at me, his eyes heavy-lidded. Bizarrely, he didn't look one bit scared. Beneath his cloak, he had pale skin and a hint of a beard.

"Who are you?" I barked, my lolly sticking out of my mouth.

He blinked down at me. "No one."

"What's your name, dimwit?"

His mouth opened and closed mutely. Then he said, "The Great Mortality is coming for us all."

And that confirmed my hunch. The jackdaws had been Baleros's work.

I pressed the blade a little harder, drawing a tiny bit of blood. "Let's just get down to brass tacks, shall we? Where do I find Baleros?"

His eyes widened—just enough to tell me that he recognized the name. Still, he didn't say anything. Why wasn't he scared of his clearly impending death?

I grabbed one of his wrists, slamming it against the wall. He grunted. The cloth slipped up his arm, and for a moment, my heart skipped a beat. There—burned into his skin—was a brand. But it wasn't Baleros's brand as I'd expected. No, this was the moon rising over a tower.

It was the symbol of the Institute. So it wasn't just the cloaks. Baleros had gone to serious lengths to frame us.

"That looks familiar," I muttered. Thing was, the Institute didn't brand people. *Baleros* branded people. I knew, because I'd once cut his brand off my own wrist.

I leaned in, sniffing the faint, electrical scent of magic.

Nearly imperceptible, a dark aura glimmered around him. What sort of enchantment was this?

"Where is he?" I hissed. "Where is Baleros?"

The man simply shook his head. "Can't tell anyone, can I?"

I reared back my arm and slammed my fist into his chin, the bone cracking as I made contact. Now, his shattered jaw hung at an angle, already swelling.

When he met my gaze, I still saw no fear there. He just stared at me, a quiet desperation in his eyes.

"How is Baleros recruiting you people?" I demanded, rage and fear rising in my chest. I could already feel myself losing control. "I need answers. Where did he find you?"

"I used to be alive." His voice sounded haunted.

I narrowed my eyes at the pulsing vein in his neck. His skin was warm, and I could hear his heart beating from here. If there's one thing I knew, it was death. And this man was not dead.

"What the hells do you mean?" I shot back. "You're still alive."

"Nah, not anymore. My name used to be Alan. I was the manager of a small sales division. An insurance company. Not only was I alive, but I was known as a bit of a party animal, as it were. Organized company footie and barbecues. Fun and games."

Oh, gods. I wished he'd just talk about torture or something.

"That was me. Right laugh," he continued in his monotone. "Before I died, I wore a boa for a laugh, made jokes about bumming the other lads. I burned my knob by sticking it in the cheese dip, and—"

I punched him hard again in the jaw. It took me a moment to realize I had no strategic reason for hitting him just then, but I didn't want to hear anything else about his life.

"You would have been my type," he said. "Pretty face, completely insane, nice set of baps—"

I hit him again. His head lolled again, and his eyelids fluttered.

"What do you mean you're dead?" I snarled. "You're objectively not dead. It's not up for argument."

"I'm dead, innit?"

Idiot. At least this explained the jackdaws' fearlessness. If a man thought he was dead, he had nothing to fear.

He stared at me. "He promised me eternal life."

"Baleros?"

"I must keep his secrets. That's the rule."

"He's not going to give you eternal life. You're not dead. You're a fucking muppet, but you're not dead. Tell me about this Great Mortality. What's the plan?"

"The dead cannot die," he said in a flat voice, blood dripping from his chin, streaming from his broken nose.

It took me a moment to hear the dim beeping noise. Another second to notice his thumb on a button, the blinking lights at his waist. And a fraction of an instant to put together that this man was about to blow himself up, with me standing next to him.

I dove away from him, landing hard on the pavement just as the bomb went off. The explosion seared my back, and shrapnel pierced the skin at my waist. I didn't want to think too long about what the shrapnel was—probably bits of Alan's bones. The explosion had temporarily deafened me, and I clamped my hands over my ears to dampen the piercing ring.

Smoke billowed around me, and I turned back to look at the man formerly known as Alan. There was hardly anything left of him, just gristle and body parts spattered over the brick and pavement.

I coughed, wincing in pain, and pushed myself up onto my hands and knees. I blocked out the vague sense that I was inhaling Alan dust, and I rubbed the smoke and grit out of my eyes. As I did, something on the pavement caught my eye —a scrap of glittering gold and green.

I crawled over to it, grunting. I picked up the colored remnant, running my fingertips over its surface. It looked like a piece of a matchbox, and the fragment read *The Skull and Cr—*

The singed edges and heat told me it had come from Alan.

My hands were shaking, and dizziness clouded my mind as I forced myself up. The jackdaw situation was worse than I thought. Somehow, Baleros was convincing people they were already dead, that serving him was the key to their eternal salvation. Not only did he have the mist army, but he'd made himself a legion of fearless human slaves.

CHAPTER 4

I rose unsteadily, leaning against a brick wall as I tried to stay standing. I'd learned a few things. But not the big question of where I'd find Baleros.

One day till the world ends.

I gripped my side, using breathing to manage the pain. The explosion had burned some of my skin, and had lacerated my back and waist.

The mournful sound of church bells knelled over the city.

I hobbled to the mouth of the alley, staring out onto the empty, darkened street.

What was he doing with the jackdaws? If there was a single piece of philosophy that guided Baleros's actions, it was the idea that chaos was the opportunity to remake the world the way he wanted it. And he was doing a bang-up job of it so far.

Amidst the city's panic, only the Institute felt calm, our walls protected by a magical moat and a river.

I touched the lumen stone at my neck, working on summoning its shadow magic. Cold power flooded my limbs, igniting my muscles. Then, I shadow-leapt down the dark street. With the tower in view, I leapt again, landing hard just before the moat of light.

A shock of pain shot up my body as I touched down before the light. I'd mistimed it a bit, landed too hard, and I was sure at least some of my limbs had been bruised in the blast.

Catching my breath, I stepped onto the bridge that spanned the magical moat. Instantly, warmth flooded me, washing over my skin. It almost felt like the light was healing me.

As I crossed the stone bridge, hunger rose in my gut. In fact, the feeling of starvation overwhelmed me so much, it eclipsed the pain of my injuries. What the hells? I'd killed the hunger gorta that once guarded the Institute. Why was I feeling this famine now?

I could think only of filling my belly, and of gnawing on the sweet, sweet grass that grew below the moat.

Furious, I jammed my hand into my bug-out bag, and I pulled out a chocolate bar and my headlamp. I flicked my headlamp on, then unwrapped the chocolate, taking a huge bite.

A cloaked fae approached me, and I just caught a glimpse of his gaunt features under his hood.

"Who are you?" I barked, furious in my hunger.

"I'm the new gorta. They're paying me double the last fella. Just doing my bit."

My stomach rumbled wildly. I clutched it, nearly doubling over. I thought Aengus had said it was nearly impossible to get a gorta.

"How's it going, then?" He pointed at my stomach. "Does the ol' belly feel a bit hollow?"

"You're not supposed to strike me," I yelled, clutching my stomach. "I'm one of the Shadow Fae. I belong here."

Ah. Right. It was hard to get a *good* gorta.

"Just want to make sure the Grand Master feels he's getting his money's worth," he said. "I've got a family to feed. Not many of you going in and out. Not many of you here, in fact. Everyone's out looking for this bogeyman. Baleros, innit. Whole place is empty."

I straightened, looking him right in the eye. "I'm here, and I'm a knight. I belong here. Let me through." I pointed out beyond the moat of magic. "I'm bleeding all over the bridge right now, having done a night's work for the Institute, and the Grand Master wants to see me."

He shrugged. "Go on, then." He jumped off the bridge to the grassy moat below.

As soon as he did, the gnawing hunger disappeared from my ribs.

I wrapped up the rest of my chocolate bar and dropped it in my bag. Then, I flicked off my headlamp, passing through the gate into the old Tower itself. My body ached in places I didn't even want to think about, and fragments of bone were embedded deep within my flesh. I winced as I walked; blood poured from my sides.

We had one day left, and only a tiny scrap of paper to go on.

As I crossed into the great hall, my body hummed at the sight of Ruadan on his rocky throne. Somehow, he looked like he'd always belonged there, as if his prior absence from its jagged contours had been a terrible error. A silver crown gleamed on his head, and the wavering torchlight gilded his perfect features—the dark eyebrows, the aggressively beautiful planes of his face.

I was so intently focused on Ruadan, I nearly missed the

king standing on the flagstones before him—and the woman by his side.

The same woman, in fact, who'd tried to kill me just a half hour ago. It was the serpent fae, smiling smugly in her red leather dress, long black hair tumbling gracefully over her shoulders. The only sign that she'd just been on a murdering binge was the glow of her body from feeding on their pain.

I limped into the room, my lip curling. "What's she doing here?"

Ruadan took in my injuries, and he tensed in his throne. His dark magic whooshed over the hall, suffocating some of the flames at the ends of the torches. For just a moment, shadows pooled in his eyes. "Are you okay?" His voice was quiet, but somehow seemed to fill the hall.

All eyes were on me, and I held my side as I walked, feeling as if I was trying to hold my body together. I'd gone a bit dizzy from the blood loss.

"I'm alive. I had some altercations." I nodded at the serpent woman. "If fact, I believe I met your friend here, earlier."

I wasn't going to mention the jackdaws in front of these strangers I didn't trust.

"How fascinating." The auburn-haired king failed to hide his irritation.

And who was *he*? Red magic glimmered and crackled around his body—not just a king, but a powerful magician.

The king turned back to Ruadan. "I don't care if you've taken him out of the dungeon. I want my son back. I am King Locrinus of Elfame, Carver of Enemies, House of the Golden Sickle, and I demand that you return Maddan to me."

Oh. Of course. He was the father of the Institute's least competent recruit, Maddan. And I suppose he wanted his son back.

Ruadan ignored the king, his eyes locked on me. He rose from his throne. "We need to speak. Privately."

The king huffed. "Honestly, what in the gods' names is this creature?"

"I'm Arianna, daughter of…. You know what? Let's not get into who sired whom. I already met Serpent Lady when she was crushing some humans to death, anyway."

As Ruadan crossed to me, he shot the serpent woman a look of such venom that I had to wonder if they had a history.

Ruadan stood over me, tugging up the edge of my shirt to inspect the damage. "How injured are you?"

"I might have bits of an insurance salesman lodged within my spleen."

"You're coming with me now."

Then, he scooped me up as if I didn't weigh a thing. His magic began snaking over my body, numbing the sharp pain and the burns. I rested my head on his chest, listening to his heartbeat.

Once we were through the archway, he whispered, "What happened?"

"First, I saw that serpent lady. The fomoire. She's vile."

Ruadan carried me up the stairs.

"Then, I found one of the jackdaws. They're definitely human, but they've been hit with a magical spell. Alan believed he was already dead. Hence, he didn't mind blowing himself up. I mean, what's the harm in blowing up when you're dead, right?"

I had a vague sense that I wasn't explaining this well, but the blood loss was starting to get to me. Leaning into Ruadan's chest, I closed my eyes.

"Everything is confusing right now, but Baleros has built himself a fearless army of humans. He's got himself a mist army, and now, an army of human suicide bombers."

At the top of the stairs, Ruadan crossed into a drafty hallway. Then, he kicked through a door. In the small, stone room, Aengus sat behind a desk, a spell book spread out in front of him.

The door slammed shut behind us.

"What's going on?" asked Aengus.

"Jackdaw bomb," I said. "They're working for Baleros, and they're now blowing themselves up."

Ruadan laid me on the desk, still cradling me against his chest.

"You're not giving that king Maddan, are you?" I asked. "Maddan's an enemy of the Institute. He's also a leaf-wearing, small-footed, dead-eyed mistake of a man."

"Quiet." Ruadan examined my waist.

"It's like the gods scrambled a person when they tried to make him."

"*Quiet.*"

Ruadan's healing magic skimmed my skin. As the pain began to seep out of my body, pleasure washed over me. Closing my eyes, I sank further against Ruadan's muscled chest, before I remembered that Aengus was watching.

I shifted on the desk, dangling my legs over the side. "Am I healed now?"

"Not exactly," he said. "I took the pain away and stopped the bleeding, but we've still got shrapnel to deal with."

I lifted a finger. "Wait. I forgot a key part of this whole situation. The jackdaws have been branded, like I was." I pointed to my wrist, where I'd cut off Baleros's brand. "But Baleros didn't brand them with his symbol. He's branded them with our symbol. He has convinced them that he will grant them eternal life as long as they do whatever he wants. I think he's going to let the Institute take the fall for his whole Great Mortality plan. He's turning the city against us."

Aengus scrubbed a hand over his chin, leaning back in his chair. "What do you think Baleros's end game is?"

"For now, the goal is to create chaos and pin the blame on us," I said. "He's trying to unsettle people. Have you see the skulls and skeletons painted on the walls around here? He really *does* have a flare for the dramatic." I tapped my fingertip to my lips as I thought. "He had this theory that the best way to take over a kingdom was to prop up a tyrant. Then, you execute the tyrant publicly. You get to look like a hero, and you rule the kingdom. And I think that's what he's doing. He's making us into the tyrants."

Ruadan crossed his arms. "People are supposed to believe those little, dead-eyed humans are Shadow Fae?"

"If humans are scared enough, they'll believe anything." I looked up into Ruadan's eyes. "He still wants that World Key on your chest. Once Baleros decides he wants something, he never lets it go. He'll want to kill you, then take your key. I don't think you should leave the Institute."

Aengus snorted. "Good luck with that advice. The fastest way to get Ruadan out of a place is to tell him that he needs to stay locked within it."

Ruadan's eyes darkened. "I'm not staying locked in here. Nearly every knight in the Institute is out there searching for Baleros, and we will be, too. We don't rest until we find him. Baleros still has my mother imprisoned somewhere, and I'm not hiding behind these walls while others try to find her and stop the Plague."

I gripped the desk hard, my thoughts muddled. "I'll take care of it."

Ruadan shook his head *no,* then added, "You can't even stand up straight. You've lost too much blood, and you have no idea where to go next."

"The clue." I reached into my pocket. "I forgot the clue. A pub called The Skull and Crossbones. It was on the jackdaw."

I didn't want this lead slipping away from me. "I think I should go there now."

"Not now." Ruadan's commanding tone rang throughout the room. "Aengus, make sure King Locrinus doesn't get into any trouble. Arianna's coming to my room."

I blinked. "What?"

He touched the small of my back, guiding me to the door. "Don't argue with me. Do you know what happens to a knight who argues with the Grand Master?" His soothing voice caressed my skin, but there was a hint of threat in it.

I followed him into the corridor, hurrying to keep up with his pace. My lip curled. "Disobeying the Grand Master? A light spanking?"

"In Emain, disobedient knights were tied naked to trees—"

"I like where you're going with this," I said.

"—they were fed meals of oatcakes and honey—"

"Literally none of this sounds bad."

"—and then wood-poppets would rise from the tree trunks and rip through their guts to get to the honey."

I winced. "That part sounds bad. What the fuck is a wood-poppet? You know what, never mind. Why are we going to your room?"

"Arianna, even if you can't feel it, you still have bits of … insurance salesman lodged in your organs."

I grimaced. "You make a good point."

"And I'm coming with you to the pub."

Obviously, I should not have told Ruadan that he needed to stay confined within the Tower, because he clearly had a contrary nature. He'd start banging on about wood-poppets again if I argued with him.

"I'm not being disobedient, but it makes no sense for you to come with me," I said. "You're the target, and Baleros can't get inside the Tower."

Dark magic snaked around him. Frost slicked the walls as we walked, and my teeth started chattering.

"You don't like feeling trapped places, do you?" I said.

"No." His eyes were straight ahead, not meeting my gaze.

"Particularly by Baleros, I'm guessing."

He didn't respond. Baleros had been my master and Ruadan's mentor centuries ago, when Ruadan was just a young fae. I knew what kind of methods Baleros used to control people.

"Did he used to lock you in an iron box?" I felt like I was entering dangerous waters, but I wanted to know more about Ruadan.

"Rock," he said. "Underground river."

Silence fell over us as we walked, but Ruadan's quiet rage had sucked nearly all the light out of the hall.

I knew one thing for certain. Like me, Ruadan would never be at ease until Baleros was in the grave for good.

CHAPTER 5

$\mathscr{I}$ sat at the edge of Ruadan's bed, and he stood over me. We had less than a day to sort out this whole situation.

"Take off your shirt," said Ruadan.

I considered making a "buy a girl dinner" joke first, but it wasn't funny, and I smothered the impulse. I kept my mouth shut and pulled off my shirt.

Ruadan sucked in a sharp breath, and I looked down at myself, craning my neck to see my wounds. When I saw the damage, I groaned. I couldn't feel it anymore, but my back and sides had been shredded and burned.

"Lie down on your front," said Ruadan.

I did as he said, folding my arms beneath my chin. I closed my eyes, feeling only faint pressure as he cleaned the wounds, pulling out the shrapnel. Because of his magic, I felt no pain.

"Don't you have healers for this?" I asked.

"We do. But they're not as thorough as I am."

"I feel privileged to be treated by the Grand Master himself." I licked my lips, daring myself to ask the question really on my mind. "With Savus dead, are you keeping that whole virginity pledge?"

"It wasn't virginity."

"Whatever. Abstinence."

"As has always been the case, Knights of the Shadow Fae may not take lovers within the Institute. They may take lovers outside the Institute. Not that any of that is my top concern at this point."

Okay. That was a very formal way of saying "you and I will never be sleeping together, so get it out of your over-heated mind."

Silence fell as he worked. Then, Ruadan said, "You died." It seemed Ruadan was not letting this little point go. "When Baleros was here, he thrust a sword into your heart. You thrust your sword into his. Both were made of iron. You both died. I know why Baleros came back to life. He pledged his soul to Emerazel, and she revives him. I do not know how you returned."

I let silence fall again. He hadn't actually asked a question, so I didn't bother answering it.

He tugged down the top of my skirt, working on the flesh over my hip.

I breathed in his smell—pine and apples. Weeks ago, I'd spent a few days naked in this bed, my body wrapped around his, writhing from an overdose of lust magic. And now, Ruadan's magic was rushing over me in tingling waves of pleasure. I couldn't see it, but I was sure my skin looked better already.

After a few more minutes of his delicious healing magic, he spoke again. "The wounds are cleaned and healed. Now tell me what you are."

Ruadan had a little habit of not answering questions that he didn't want to answer. A brilliant tactic in its simplicity. He just kept his mouth shut and that was that. I had another brilliant tactic up my sleeve. Instead of answering, I turned over onto my back, one hand slung over my breasts, but leaving one of my nipples in view as if by accident.

I blinked at him innocently. "What was the question?"

Black slammed into his eyes, his demonic form taking over. For just an instant, I caught a glimpse of phantom wings sweeping down from behind his shoulders. *Ahh ... there's the incubus.*

My breath caught in my throat. I'd never seen those before. Still, he hadn't fully shifted yet. If he did, I didn't imagine his incubus side had much self-restraint.

He planted his hands on either side of my head, boxing me in, and warmth pulsed through my belly. Slowly, he raked his gaze up and down my body, lingering on my bare breasts, swooping down my waist, my hips, between my legs. The look he was giving me was purely carnal, like he wanted to devour me completely.

Lightning-fast, he leaned down, his breath warming my neck. He inhaled deeply, growling in a low timbre that reverberated through my gut. My back started to arch, and I let my arm fall away from my breasts completely. I licked my lips, staring into his dark eyes. He gripped the sheets so tightly his muscles were shaking.

It took him a moment to master control of himself, until at last, his eyes returned to violet.

Damn.

He pushed himself up, turning away from me.

I let out a long, slow exhale, staring at his muscled back.

"Rest for an hour," he said. "Then, we're leaving for The Skull and Crossbones."

* * *

AFTER ABOUT TWENTY minutes of resting, I hopped out of

bed. I snatched a change of clothes out of my bug-out bag—a white button-down dress. It looked absurdly innocent—perfect for undercover missions, since the Shadow Fae never dressed in white.

I pulled it on and grabbed my bug-out bag. Then, I armed myself with one of the swords and sheaths from Ruadan's wall. I headed out to the courtyard.

Before leaving for a mission, I liked to spend a little time delving into research at the library—even more so now that my friend Melusine worked there.

Fully healed now, I moved rapidly up the stairs to the dim light of the library. There, I found Melusine perched on a ladder, nose in a book about unicorn shifters. A glow worm illuminated the air above her with golden light. She didn't seem to notice me stride in.

"Melusine."

She jumped, slamming the book shut. It took me a moment to recognize the flushed look on her face, and the heated look in her eyes, and to realize that Melusine had a bit of a thing for unicorn shifters. Interesting.

"I wasn't thinking about anything weird!" she blurted. "It says here in the literature that there's nothing wrong with someone reading a simple, educational book about muscular men growing hooves and a horn."

"Simmer down, Melusine. I just need some help learning about a particular type of magic."

She nodded, straightening her dress. "What can you tell me about this particular type of magic?"

"You ever heard of something where a human thinks he's dead, but he's not?"

"Like he's physically fine, but he's all screwed up in the head?"

"Yeah."

She scratched her head. "It sounds like psychomancy. It's

a new type of magic, about a hundred years old. You know, when I hear about people thinking something that's not real, I think *delusions*. I put two and two together. Right? I once had a delusion that my brother's toy soldiers were trying to kill me with poison. But it was actually our cat. Do you know what I mean?"

Nope. "Sure. Yes."

She began leading me to an alcove in another corner of the library.

"What did you call it?" I asked. "Psycho-something?"

"The psychomancers were influenced by the human field of psychology. It's a fascinating field. I know at least several hundred things about it." She pushed her glasses up on her nose. "Some psychomancers are able to meddle with human minds in ways that mimic actual human delusions."

She pulled a book off a shelf and began paging through it, humming to herself quietly as she did. At last, she stopped on a page, her face brightening.

"Here we go. Cotard Syndrome. Person thinks he's decaying, sometimes that he's in hell. Total shock to the system, really. It can be caused by brain damage." She shut the book. "Or, in this case, magic."

I crossed my arms. "It makes a weird sort of sense. The jackdaws are fearless, and Baleros is using them to frame us." I bit my lip. "And what can you tell me about the Black Death?"

"That one's easy. Humans ascribe it to a bacterium, but it was actually caused by magic. Legend says the Horseman of Death caused it."

My throat tightened. "What?"

"That's the legend. Big outbreaks in the sixth century, the fourteenth, the seventeenth. Streets filled with bodies, red crosses on the doors, stench of death everywhere. Real fun, you know? Tell you the truth, some *did* have real fun.

36

Did you know that people reacted in two ways? They flogged themselves in the streets, or they fornicated everywhere."

I nodded. That actually made sense. From my experience, humans were obsessed with precisely two things: shagging and hating themselves for shagging.

"Whips and sexual relations all over the place," she added.

"I've been to a party like that."

Melusine shrugged. "I don't know a lot about romance, per se, but plague-infested London doesn't seem like a romantic setting to me. Bleeding neck buboes, red crosses on the doors, rats feasting on the dead. Is that something humans find sexually stimulating, like a man staring at an attractive brassiere in a catalogue? I've got no idea. That part's not in the literature. To be frank, I don't understand humans or people in general. But maybe they figured they had to make the most of their lives."

I nodded. "Okay, I get the idea."

"Why are you asking about the Plague?"

"Oh, um, maybe I should have led with that. We have less than a day until everyone in London gets the Plague and the world ends."

"Ah."

"I expected a bit more of a reaction."

She frowned. "I mean, the Plague sounds bad, but the world won't end."

"The world has ended before," I countered, vaguely aware of the absurdity of my argument.

"Not really, since we're still here."

"Right." I chewed my lip. "I see your point. Melusine, what the hells is a wood-poppet?"

"A wood-poppet? I've never heard of that."

Had Ruadan been messing with me?

A loud boom interrupted our conversation, and the floor

beneath us shook. Books tumbled off the shelves, and I covered my head with my arms. "What the hells?" I shouted.

Melusine—cleverly—had immediately leapt to an archway, avoiding the falling books.

"Gods below," I grunted. I clutched the bookshelf as the floor stabilized. "That's the second explosion tonight."

"Someone's attacking the Institute," added Melusine, rather unnecessarily.

I pulled out my sword, summoning my shadow magic. It whispered through my veins, cold and electric. I began shadow-leaping, rushing through the air, down the stairs. I slammed through the Tower door, then shadow-leapt across the Tower Green. Smoke curled into the air from one of the Towers.

As I shadow-leapt, the wind whipped at my lavender hair. Blurs of movement whisked across the green as the other Knights of the Shadow Fae leapt into action, moving for the battlements.

I leapt up to the top of the tower walkway, slamming down hard on the stone. My heart hammered against my ribs as the smell of smoke thickened around me. From the inner wall, I leapt over the stony gap, my sword already drawn. I hurtled through the air to the exterior tower wall.

I landed on a walkway that loomed over the Thames. The golden moat beamed below. From the ground, dark smoke billowed into the night sky.

At the top of the barbican, I stared down at the gaping hole in the stone wall below me—and the ragged gap in the moat's golden light. Glittering red magic shimmered in the air. Two humans lay injured on the pavement—a man and a woman, clothing torn, bodies bloodied. Rubble littered the ground around them.

The wind tore at my hair, and I frantically scanned the dark river, looking for signs of our attacker. City lights glistened on the water, but I couldn't see anything resembling an assailant.

Ruadan landed next to me on the battlement, and he gripped the side of the wall as he looked out onto the river. His dark magic lashed the air around him.

Then, cold air whooshed past me as he leapt to the pavement below. Gripping my sword, I summoned my lumen stone's power and leapt down by his side, landing hard on the stony debris. The shock of the impact shot through my shins.

I turned to survey the damage. The explosion had ripped through the exterior wall into a sparsely furnished room.

"This is precisely where we'd been keeping Maddan," Ruadan growled. He whirled, scanning the horizon for the ginger prince. "He's gone. He shadow-leapt away."

"How?" I asked. "He didn't have a lumen crystal." But even as the words were out of my mouth, I was beginning to understand. "Baleros has one, though."

Ruadan reached out, skimming his fingertips over the glittering red magic.

My fists tightened. "How could he possibly break through the magical moat? I thought it was impenetrable."

"It is," said Ruadan. "From the outside."

Unfortunately for us, Maddan's father had been *inside* the fortress.

I scanned the debris, my gaze roaming over glistening pieces of flesh, a fragment of bone…. A passerby caught in the wrong place?

No.

A dark scrap in the rubble caught my eye. I reached down, picking up a tattered bit of black cloth. The coarse wool felt just like the fabric worn by the other jackdaw, edges singed.

"This was a coordinated attack," I said. "The king on the

inside to pull down the moat, a jackdaw on the outside to blow himself up. Someone here at the right time to deliver the lumen stone. But why would Baleros care about Maddan?"

"He doesn't," said Ruadan. "You know how he thinks."

Baleros's twenty-fifth law of power: Divide and conquer.

"Of course," I said. "He's trying to sow division. It's hard to fight a battle on two fronts. If you get sidetracked by fighting the small-footed prince and his father, you'll be vulnerable. Don't let Baleros distract you."

Ruadan's magic iced the air around him until my breath frosted in front of my face. "His distractions won't work. We're staying focused on Baleros. I'll have our mages restore the moat."

I hugged myself. "How long will that take?"

"Could be a few days."

"Shit. He's leaving us vulnerable while we try to hunt him down. You've got the knights roaming all over London looking for him, and he wants you to call them back here to defend the Institute."

"I'm not doing that. The Institute can stay vulnerable. Right now, you and I are leaving for The Skull and Crossbones."

CHAPTER 6

*I*n my little white dress, I gripped the straps of my bug-out bag as we skulked down Crutched Friars. The night air skimmed over my bare arms and legs, tension hunched my shoulders, and I kept looking behind me. At any moment, another jackdaw might run out of an alley to blow himself up.

We now had about twenty-one hours left until everyone died of the Plague.

"Gods, I want a whiskey," I muttered.

Ruadan let the comment hang in the air. One of these days, I was going to get him drunk, assuming that was even possible.

As we walked, he loomed over me, his silhouette indistinct. He was doing his *wraith* thing where you couldn't really see his outline.

I swallowed hard. Twenty-one hours until rotting bodies filled the streets, eaten by rats....

The hair stood up on my nape. Around the Institute, the roads were eerily empty tonight. These streets were thousands of years old, with strange names like Savage Gardens and Seething Lane. For thousands of years, the streets had teemed with people. Not now.

We walked down the long, curving road called Crutched Friars. These streets had been around the *first* time the Great Mortality had hit the city. What stories these streets would have to tell—ancient as Baleros. Older than the Wraith….

Shadows climbed the walls around us as Ruadan kept us hidden with his magic. What stories did *he* have to tell after all these centuries?

"How old are you, exactly?"

"What difference does it make? That has no bearing on Baleros."

"That vampire woman, Elise, said six hundred." I plowed right on. "Is that true?"

"Six-hundred ninety-six."

"That's bloody ancient. Surely you need to go to bed at seven-thirty, after a quiet night of soaking your feet and watching gardening shows."

He grunted.

I couldn't do the mental math, exactly, but I thought he was born sometime in the thirteen hundreds. "So you were around when the Great Mortality hit? The big one? The fourteenth century one?"

"Yes." His dark magic snaked over my skin. "It seemed as if the world was ending."

I swallowed hard. "How often did you leave Emain to come to London?"

"Once I escaped some of my training with Baleros, I was married here in London."

"How old were you when you joined the Shadow Fae?"

"I was raised among them from birth."

My blood stirred. A rare flash of openness from Ruadan, but these memories didn't seem like happy ones. Cold magic poured off him, rushing over my skin.

I should have left it there, should have heeded the warning—the air frosting, the shadows thickening. But I had to know more.

"What happened to your wife?"

"She died."

"How?" I'd missed some tact with my question, like telling him I was sorry for his loss.

"Killed by Adonis. Horseman of Death."

His words slid over my skin like cold rain. "Oh?"

"I'm almost positive, yes."

"But you're not entirely sure?"

"I'm certain that a monstrous creature like him doesn't belong on Earth."

"But aren't many of us monsters in our own way?"

He narrowed his eyes. "Along with the other horsemen, he created the apocalypse twenty-five years ago."

"But I thought he worked to stop it. He fought *against* the Horsemen of Pestilence and War. He tried to stop all the destruction. At least, that's what I heard."

"In the end, yes. But his very presence on Earth led to it. Without him, none of that would have happened. Not to mention the fact that he can still slaughter entire populations just by losing his temper. I think he was responsible for the Black Plague."

"But you don't *know* that he was."

"And he's probably responsible for this most recent plague in the Isle of Dogs. He is Death, and he has no place here."

I fell silent.

"I can hear your heart racing," Ruadan said quietly. "Why?"

"I'm just wary, that's all. There could be jackdaws with explosive vests in any of these alleyways. Anyway, my point was—Baleros seems to be drawing from the old days. The

43

Plague stuff, the skeleton murals, the cloaks. You and Baleros were both alive then. I wasn't. What was London like in those days?"

"Is there a point to this?"

"We're undercover. We're supposed to be blending in. I'm not sure if you've ever spent time around normal people in your six hundred ninety-four years of life, but they do this thing called chitchat. They talk about the weather, or sports, or the mystery persons who stole their cheese at work."

He shot me a sharp look. "That's asinine."

I loosed a sigh. "Well, when we get into The Skull and Crossbones, how about you let me do the talking? We don't need Baleros tracking our movements, and you don't have a chance in seven hells of blending in. And anyway, that time period seems to interest Baleros. Maybe it's important. Maybe he liked his life back then."

Shadows snaked around us, and the silence stretched out for so long that I was certain the conversation was over. At last, he said, "London was full of death and beauty. Elegance and depravity." His gaze flicked to mine for a long moment, and I had the inexplicable sense he was talking about me. "An intoxicating combination."

A smile curled my lips. "More details, please."

"Murders, executions. Towering, spindly churches that reached for the heavens. Human heads on pikes. Pageants, maypoles. Claret and beer. A royal menagerie with lions and bears. On this road, a king marched his brother's mistress through the streets half-naked as penance for her sins. Her hair was golden in the sunlight. Those with strength ruled. Kings led their troops into battle. And most of all—chaos and death ruled the streets."

"Ah. And there's our answer. Chaos. What a glorious time for Baleros."

Captivated, I was about to push for more information,

but Ruadan stopped walking. His violet eyes burned as he stared across the street. I turned, catching sight of what he was looking at.

A mural of black and ivory with splashes of red—skeletons dancing with kings, queens, and soldiers. And behind the skeletons lurked cloaked men. Jackdaws. No. Not jackdaws … I think they were … were they supposed to be us?

"There's another one of his murals," I muttered.

"The Great Mortality." Silver flashed in Ruadan's eyes. "Those pictures were everywhere once."

I scrubbed a hand over my mouth. "Could be a message for us. A reminder. We have just over a day to deliver you, or he unleashes the godsdamned Plague."

Ruadan cocked his head. "He already delivered that message. What else?"

I felt like I was being tested here. I closed my eyes for a moment, trying to get in Baleros's mind.

Baleros's twenty-fourth rule of power: Win their hearts by slaughtering their oppressor.

"Frightened people are easier to control. When the humans are scared enough, they'll turn on us. When Baleros kills you in a giant spectacle, they'll be thankful. It's quite brilliant, really."

"Brilliant," he repeated.

"I mean, he is very good at planning ahead."

Ruadan started walking again, fog and shadows curling around him, until he reached a blank brick wall. He halted, staring at it. It took me a moment to register the faint gleam of magic that shimmered over the wall. A glimmering red—the same color as the magic we'd seen at the Institute.

The wall was glamoured, and the magic belonged to King Locrinus.

Ruadan reached out, stroking his fingertips over the wall, and the glamour fell away. Now, we stood before a warped wooden door. Just above us, a pub sign creaked forlornly in the breeze—an ivory skull and crossbones on black paint.

Ruadan pushed through the door, into a pub where candlelight wavered over crooked stone walls and oak benches. The stone walls were hung with stags' antlers, skulls, and framed pages from alchemical texts.

Three humans sat at a table, dressed in black cloaks and star-flecked wizard hats. They hunched over tiny, pewter figurines and colored dice. A human man with long, blond hair in a ponytail rose, knocking over his chair. "I am Boradrion, Dark Fae Lord of Hellbania! I will smiteth mine porcine enemy with a roll of—" He rolled the die across the table.

A bearded man sighed loudly through his nose. "You rolled a natural one. The boar bites your dick off."

Boradrion's face reddened. "Methrior rocked the table with his meaty dwarf hands!" He slammed his fists on the table. "I need a re-roll. Dungeon Master Ethan, this is bollocks."

"What the hells," I muttered.

My heart sank. I'd kind of been hoping for a good fight, but I would not find that here. And yet … *someone* with magic had glamoured the door. Maybe they were more powerful than they appeared.

It was at this point that Boradrion of the Ponytail realized we'd come in, and he pushed his glasses up on his nose. His face still looked pinched and red. "Who enters The Skull and Crossbones?"

Baleros's third law of power: Always let your enemy underestimate you.

I blinked. "Yeah, so, like, this door just kinda appeared in the wall? It was kind of weird." An American accent again. Always with the American accents. "And it looked like magic or something? And so we just came inside. You know what I mean? Do you guys have vodka and Red Bull?"

Boradrion glowered at me, then turned to his friend. "Gods *damn* it, Methrior. I told you the glamour wouldn't hold. You're a terrible mage."

Methrior scooted out from the booth, glowering through his spectacles. "I thought it was a solid spell," he said quietly. "King Locrinus helped me with it."

Did he, now? Quite the little alliance Maddan's father had formed with Baleros and his human idiot crew.

Still, no one had noticed Ruadan. With his Wraith fog around him, people just didn't see him.

I cocked my head. "You guys seem to know a lot about magic and stuff."

Methrior's chest puffed. "I'm being instructed by a real fae king."

The bearded man—Dungeon Master Ethan—strode up behind Methrior, wiggling his fingers. "He's not the only one. Watch this. *Ekkimu.*" Red light glowed from his fingertips, and he grinned.

Methrior grunted with disapproval. "Yes, but he's spent more time on me, because he has recognized my innate talent. I can do real attack spells now. Look." Methrior lifted his hand, staring at his fingertips. "*Baraqu!*"

Lightning shot from his fingertips, striking the ceiling. Instantly, the wood ignited, flames roaring above us.

Boradrion covered his head with his arms. "Put the fire out, you bloody donkey! I told you to stop doing that inside."

Coughing, Methrior called out, "*Malititu!*"

Water rushed down from the ceiling, quenching the fire. It soaked my hair and my clothing before petering out to a brown trickle. I stopped myself from kicking the living shite out of all of them.

With water dripping off me, I widened my eyes. "Amazing. How did you get a fae king to instruct you?"

"Something big is coming," said Boradrion. "A reckoning. Something that will change the world we know. And we're the foot soldiers. When the change comes, we will rule by his side."

Sure you will, fuckwit. I licked my lips, shivering a little in my sodden clothes. "What's coming, then?"

"The Great Mortality will come for us all. Death, the great leveler. Corpses will litter London's streets once more, bodies falling so fast there will be no time to bury the dead. Only those with magic will survive. Or those we take under our protection. You have but one more day to make the most of your existence before you begin to rot." He cocked his head, grinning. "Unless you want to join us as our serving wench. If you would like to come to my abode for cheese sandwiches and some sexual intercourse I would be happy to oblige."

The mage rolls a critical failure, no charisma modifier. The serving wench imagines ripping off his head at the neck.

I pouted. "But I thought a boar bit your dick off?" Wrong move, but I couldn't help myself.

His face reddened. "I assure you, everything is in working order."

"I'll think about it." *Or, more accurately, I'd sooner be buried in the earth up to my neck and pelted to death with twenty-sided dice.* I crossed my arms. "And while I'm thinking about that tempting possibility, can you tell me how the Great Mortality will come to London?"

CHAPTER 7

*B*oradrion's eyes shone. "*He* will bring it. And I am his soldier." His eyes widened, and he took a step closer. He pulled up his cowl, which got caught for a moment on his ponytail.

Now we were getting somewhere, and there was no doubt in my mind that he was talking about Baleros. "And where do we find him? If I wanted to serve him, too?"

Boradrion tapped his fingers on his arms, wrinkling his nose. "I'm not supposed to tell anyone that. Not even sexy wenches."

"Where is your leader?" Ruadan's voice rumbled through the room.

Boradrion's beady eyes shifted to Ruadan, his body tensing. "What the hells? I didn't notice that one, did you, Methrior? He's bloody enormous." He stepped closer, squinting as he tried to home in on Ruadan. "Are you…. Are you *fae*? Are you the Wraith?"

He'd just signed his own death warrant with that realization. Now, there was no way we could leave these three alive.

In a blur of black smoke, Ruadan shifted. Within the next

heartbeat, he was gripping Boradrion by the throat, lifting him off the ground. "Tell us where we find Baleros, or I crush this one's throat."

Boradrion kicked helplessly at the air, his eyes bulging.

Methrior began chanting in Angelic, and a ball of fire glowed in his hand. Dungeon Master Ethan chanted right along with him.

Maybe we would be getting that fight after all.

"*Edin Na Zu!*" Methrior screeched, fiery magic blazing from his fingertips.

I pulled my dagger from its sheath just as Methrior screamed the final word of his spell—*Iddimu*--and red magic exploded from his body.

The magic slammed into my chest, and I lost control of the knife. I hit the ground hard, with a loud crack. The force of the magic had knocked the wind out of me. On the ground, I grimaced, fairly certain he'd cracked my ribs.

My gaze flicked to Ruadan across the pub, and it seemed like he'd taken the brunt of the attack. His body had cracked a stone wall.

I could feel his rage from here. In fact, his eyes had turned completely black. Shadows billowed around him, expanding and contracting like lungs. Ice frosted the air, the temperature breaking some of the glass bottles. Looking at Ruadan with his nightmarish face on was like looking into the void itself. And he hadn't even fully shifted yet. No, I was only seeing the phantom wings behind him.

"Methrior!" Boradrion yelped. "It's an incubus. Do you know what happens when an incubus loses control?"

My ears perked up. *I* didn't know what happened when an incubus lost control.

A low growl boomed around the room, and ice spread across the floor. Ruadan stared at Methrior and flicked his wrist. I gaped in fascinated horror as Methrior's body split in two, starting at the crown and splitting downward, the man screaming until his mouth and throat had been ripped apart. The other two humans began screaming, their hysteria deafening.

My blood boomed through my veins. Ruadan was more terrifying than I'd imagined.

And yet still, Ruadan seemed perfectly in control, his muscles tightly coiled. I'm not sure I even wanted to imagine what he'd look like out of control….

I grunted, willing myself to roll over on all fours. Pain shot through my ribs, but I kept my eye on Boradrion.

He clutched his throat, wincing. "Get them out of here," he rasped. His face reddened, "Dungeon Master Ethan, get them out of here!"

Ethan was trying to chant again, but I could tell he was stumbling over his words, panicking. The temperature in the room plummeted further, my breath misting in front of my face. Then, dark magic snaked across the room from Ruadan's fingertips. From the magical tendrils, thorny spikes dug into Boradrion's flesh.

Slowly, with pain splintering my ribs, I pushed myself up.

"Where is Baleros keeping Queen Macha?" Ruadan spoke quietly, but his voice seemed to boom around the room, echoing in my skull.

Blood dripped from Boradrion's punctured skin, the magical thorns digging in deeper. "I don't know where she is!" he shrieked. "Ethan! Ethan I will light your fucking dice on fire if you do not kill him!"

"Where is Baleros?" The quiet control in Ruadan's voice sent tremors up my spine.

Dungeon Master Ethan tried to chant, stuttering in a panic. His face had gone completely white. He had about four seconds before he just passed out.

I scrambled for my knife, wincing as I snatched it off the

ground. At last, Ethan managed to summon a red ball of magic.

He tossed the ball of fire just as I leapt across the room. I touched down behind him and held the blade to his throat, nicking the skin just a little. The bastard was taller than me and the angle wasn't easy.

Electric magic crackled the air, and the hair began standing up on my nape. I couldn't fight with magic. All I could do was leap away and try to avoid it.

"We're done playing," I said sweetly. They were all going to die. "Tell us where to find your leader, or I'll make sure you suffer at the end."

I could feel Ethan's body trembling. Good. If he was scared, he'd do what I asked. "You don't understand," he stammered.

"Oh, I understand. If you don't give us the information we're looking for, I will gut you right here. I don't usually like to kill humans. It's not a fair fight. But you made a very bad choice when you decided to work for Baleros, so I won't feel bad."

"*Edin Na Zu!*" he shouted, and magic crackled up his spine, searing me.

I pulled my hand away, then lunged forward and stabbed him in the shoulder before he could continue the spell. He screamed.

"What did I tell you?" I shouted. His blood had spattered over my sodden clothes. "I told you I would hurt you. And you saw what Ruadan just did to your friend, didn't you? That was bloody terrifying. I think we can all agree on that point."

Ethan turned to me, his face pale, streaked with tears. "Stop hurting me!"

"I will. Just tell me where to find Baleros, and you can be on your way."

The sounds of Boradrion's screaming echoed off the walls. Still, no one was giving up their leader.

Ethan stammered, "*Edin Na—*"

I caught him in the left shoulder with the blade, and he fell to his knees, wailing. Why was he protecting Baleros with his life? These three didn't seem like the most loyal and courageous of men.

"Stop!" shrieked Ethan. "I don't know where he is. He has three generals. They're the only ones who know. One of them is meeting now—"

"Don't you tell her, Ethan!" Boradrion screamed. "You know what he'll do to us!"

Ethan sobbed, "*Edin Na—*"

I kicked him hard in the chest, and he fell backward onto the wood floor. Blood pooled around him.

"Where do I find the generals?"

"Meeting now. Skull and Crossbones…" he muttered.

"But *this* is The Skull and Crossbones…."

"*Edin Na Zu!*"

A ball of magic slammed into my thigh and pain rocketed up my hip. Another caught me in the side and agony danced up my spine. I landed hard on my back again, all the wind knocked out of me. Apparently, Dungeon Master Ethan was finding his mojo again in his last moments on earth.

"*Edin Na—*" Ethan bellowed.

Dark magic shot out of Ruadan's fingertips, winding around Ethan. It bound his arms to his body, lashing his skin with thorns of magic. They sliced deeper into the human's flesh, flaying him.

My stomach turned. I'd never seen Ruadan unleash his most terrifying abilities before, and I had a feeling this was only the tip of the iceberg.

"You're not going to win this battle," Ruadan growled.

Frost and ice spread out over the floor, and my teeth chattered. Ruadan and his godsdamned rage ice.

"You don't understand!" Ethan sobbed. "Whatever you do to us, it won't be as bad as what *he* would do!"

Morbid curiosity got the better of me. "What would he do?"

"Unspeakable torture; bodies broken, flayed, then healed again. Over and over." Ethan's words were nearly incomprehensible in his panic. "Then, turned into jackdaws."

Ruadan cut me a sharp look, one that said "prepare yourself." Except I didn't know for what, which made the warning a bit pointless.

Before I could so much as grip the back of a chair, darkness descended, blooming from inside my mind until it coated my skull. Terror slammed into me like an oncoming train.

I'd been hit with a little dose of Ruadan's fear magic, and I wasn't good at withstanding it. Adrenaline shot along my veins, and the wood floor fell out from beneath my feet.

CHAPTER 8

*M*y bare feet pounded the forest's soil, snapping twigs. The scent of death filled the air. I knew what I'd see when I got to the forest's edge. Bile rose in my throat as I peered out from behind an oak.

He'd done this. My father. He'd killed them all.

I'd seen her red hair splayed out over the ground, the blood pouring from my mum's mouth.

Darkness washed over me like ink. He killed her.

No. No.... That's not what happened.

This time, a new thought hammered in the back of my skull, a shrieking staccato note I tried to block out.... The terrible truth I'd been running from.

That's not what really happened.

Screaming pierced my mind, drowning out all other thoughts.

I was horrified to realize it was my own.

The vision cleared, and I found myself on the floor of the pub, hunched over on my hands and knees. Nausea climbed up my throat, and I vomited onto the hardwood floor, my entire body shaking. The sickness had been rising in me for a while now, since I'd seen Ruadan rip a man in two with just a flick of his wrist. The memory of my mum's death had pushed me over the edge.

I'd stopped screaming, but the shrieks continued in my mind.

Luckily, there hadn't been much in my stomach, since I'd already puked once tonight. I scrubbed my hand across my mouth, more than a little mortified that Ruadan was here to watch me throw up from fear.

Had the humans spoken? Had they given up their master? I had no idea, because I'd been busy throwing up on the floorboards.

Thanks for that, Ruadan. Arsehole.

When I looked up again, the shrieking in my skull had started to fade.

"Three generals! Three generals!" Ethan shouted, nearly incoherent. "Look for The Skull and Crossbones!"

"Ethan, no!" shouted Boradrion. That's when I saw the tiny, red button dangling from his keychain.

"Bomb!" I shouted.

I didn't even see Ruadan move, just felt the force of him slam into me, then us hurtling across the room. The wooden door splintered into shards as our bodies made impact. At this point, it felt as if my ribs had been cracked in multiple places.

We crashed onto the ground outside just as the bomb went off, and my bones took another blow from the pavement.

Ruadan's heavy body covered me, practically crushing me. Heat from the explosion seared the sides of my arms, glass and wood raining all around us. I coughed onto the ground as the initial blast receded.

I gasped for breath. It took me a moment to realize the flames had disappeared completely—no sign of an explosion whatsoever. My chest heaved, and Ruadan slowly shifted his enormous weight off of me. When I craned my neck to look back at the pub, it wasn't destroyed as I had expected.

Wincing from my broken ribs, I stared at the wooden walls and glass windows—all completely intact once more. The only thing that looked different about it was the crackle of glittering red magic before the pub's dark facade.

Then, a hot shock of pain, a shard piercing my chest. It took me a moment to realize what had happened—that one of my broken ribs had punctured my lungs.

I gasped, momentarily unable to speak from the pain. Ruadan whirled back to face me, crouching down by my side. Agony speared my chest.

"Where does it hurt?" he asked.

"Ribs," I gritted out.

Ruadan's fingers slid inside my damp shirt, his magic already meandering up my chest. As it skimmed over my body, my muscles began to unclench, the pain ebbing from my bones. Strange that someone with such intense healing powers could also rip a man in two the way he had. Ruadan, demigod of the night, could be either the most beautiful dream or the most terrifying nightmare, depending on how he felt about you.

Which was exactly why I couldn't let my secret get out.

As the pain left me, I breathed out slowly, my mind flickering with the image of red hair spread out over dirt. That memory….

Anger started to simmer. What right did Ruadan have to screw with my mind like that?

"Better?" he asked, his violet eyes shining with genuine concern.

"Fine," I said, a hint of anger in my voice. "But we have to find the generals they were talking about."

I pushed myself up, my body groaning as I crossed to the pub door.

I pulled the door open, finding that the pub looked much as it had when we'd first come in. Except now, three human bodies lay on the floor—two of them surprisingly intact, considering the explosion they'd just endured. Only Methrior lay ripped apart, courtesy of my charming mentor.

I hurried over to Ethan and put my fingers to his throat to feel for a pulse. Nothing—no breath, no heart pumping.

Death came for them. Death will come for me.

I clamped my hands over my ears as if trying to drown out my own thoughts. Ruadan had *really* screwed with my mind.

Ruadan's eyes pierced the pub's gloom as he studied me. "What's wrong with you?"

"You shouldn't toy with people's heads and expect them to carry on like normal," I snapped. "You don't know what you're messing with." *I will kill you all....*

Ruadan had gone completely still. "No, I don't, because you haven't told me. What are you?"

This conversation had taken a dangerous turn. "I'm someone who's good at killing, Ruadan," I said grimly. "That's why you recruited me."

"I recruited you because I thought you'd lead me to Baleros," he corrected me, but his attention was already shifting somewhere else.

I leapt over the bar to where they kept the alcohol, eager for a little buzz to calm my nerves. I snatched a bottle of Johnnie Walker off the shelf and unscrewed the top. I drank straight from the bottle, the booze burning my throat deliciously as it went down.

When I looked back at Ruadan, his violet eyes pierced me to the core. "You will never defeat Baleros as long as you're running from yourself."

But Ruadan, my beauty, a sane person runs from a monster.

"Can we skip the psychoanalysis?" I took another sip of whiskey.

His gaze flicked to the wall above an old, stone fireplace.

"What were you looking at?" I came out from behind the bar and glanced in the same direction.

There, on top of the pub's fireplace, sat a skull and cross-bones. Three skulls, in fact, grinning and gaping-eyed. Bizarrely, one of them wore a victory wreath. The text beneath the skulls read *Mors mihi lucrum.*

"Any idea what that means?" I asked.

"*Death is my reward.*"

I shivered. "What is it?"

"Copied from a cemetery gate nearby. St. Olave's. The place is crammed with corpses from one of London's plagues."

The date carved below the skulls read *1656.*

"What does it mean, *death is my reward?*"

"It's the motto of those who worship Adonis, Horseman of Death. They worship Thanatos."

My fingers tightened around the bottle. "His true name."

"How did you know that?"

"I heard it somewhere," I mumbled.

"I think he's working with Baleros."

A long, long sip of the whiskey. "He's on your kill list, right? I saw it."

"He is. And his kin."

Slow, steady breaths. "Why didn't you ever go back for him, to kill him? The Horseman of Death?"

"I needed two things to kill him. Stones from the Old Gods, and an immortal army to help me capture him. I have the stones already. As soon as I kill Baleros, I'll have my immortal army." Ruadan crossed his arms. "We might meet him soon."

"What makes you say that?"

"Like I said, he's the one with the power to spread the Plague. And what's more, the skeleton mural was a favorite of the death cultists. St. Olave's Cemetery was one of their meeting spots."

I sucked a steadying breath. "Baleros would never allow his followers to worship anyone but him. If I had to guess, he's simply forming his own death cult. He's the god. That's how it always is with him."

Ruadan stared at me for an uncomfortably long time, and I felt as if his gaze were seeing right into my soul.

Then, he turned and started pulling a cloak off one of the bodies. "We'll go disguised as Adonis's followers. We'll find Baleros's generals. They'll lead us to him."

CHAPTER 9

*D*ressed in stolen cloaks, we arrived at St. Olave's Cemetery.

Dread twisted through me at the sight of the cemetery entrance. Fog swept in front of the old stone archway. Spikes jutted out above the ancient gate. A total of five skulls stared out at us from the top of the arch, three of them arranged just like the carving in the pub. Here, again, we found the Latin inscription—*Death is my reward.*

Worshipers of the Horseman of Death.

Ruadan leaned down to whisper in my ear. "First, we gather information. We need to learn exactly what's going on here. Maybe we'll find out about Adonis. Don't draw blood until we need to. Understood?"

"Got it."

I was starting to notice that Ruadan often felt the need to tell me, "Don't start killing people right away."

From the gated churchyard, deep and rhythmic chanting floated through the air. A gust of cold wind rushed into my cloak, and the iron gate creaked open, welcoming us like a beckoning hand. We crossed through the archway, hoods over our heads.

Just as Boradrion had said, a meeting was taking place here. A crowd of men in cloaks stood in the center of the old churchyard, holding torches aloft and chanting. I distinctly caught the word *Thanatos*.

Would he be here? The Horseman of Death himself?

Inside the gates, the grassy ground was several feet higher than street level, and it took me a moment to realize why this was. Layers upon layers of bodies lay below us—the perfect place to worship Thanatos. Among the grass and trees, graves jutted from the ground.

No one seemed to notice us as we blended into the cloaked crowd.

At the far end of the churchyard stood a broad-shouldered man, over six feet tall. A tendril of fear coiled through me. Could that be him—the Horseman of Death, standing before us?

The crowd chanted his name, voices rising.

Their leader reached for his cowl, and my heart clenched. But when he slipped off the hood, I caught a glimpse of red horns. I let out a long, slow breath. Torchlight danced over a demon's sinewy features, and magic rippled off him, humming and buzzing over my body. Not the Horseman of Death.

I sniffed the air. From what I could tell, everyone else besides the horned demon was human.

Glowing with magic, the leader lifted his arms above his head and bellowed into the air, "We gather here to worship Thanatos!"

Gods almighty.

"Lord Gamigin, our leader!" the crowd chanted. "We gather here to worship the Lord of Death, Thanatos!"

Lord Gamigin spread out his arms. "We gather here to

offer a sacrifice."

Please tell me it's not a virgin, unless it's one of Boradrion's friends....

From the shadows, a goat bleated. A human hunched over, leading the goat into the cemetery. The goat bucked, and the man struggled for control of its neck.

Lord Gamigin tutted. "Honestly, Gerard. Get control of that thing. Thanatos demands his blood sacrifices."

Gerard grunted as the goat kicked itself free, then barreled head-first into one of the cultists, knocking him over. The crowd parted as the goat sprinted out of the churchyard, onto the street.

Silence fell over the churchyard once more.

Gerard held up his hands. "Sorry, everyone. Bit of a difficult goat, that one. I'll sedate him next time."

"Never mind," Lord Gamigin's voice boomed. "For centuries, the Horseman of Death has filled this cemetery with corpses. The Romans knew him as Dis Pater. Others know him as Adonis. We know him as Thanatos. He has left behind his legacy. The weak fear mortality; the powerful worship it. Only through death do mortal lives have meaning! Only through death are you granted a release from the torments of this world. All gods seek to rule the dominion of death. Only Thanatos does. Death is our reward!"

A voice in the back of my mind whispered, *Monster....*

Damp, frigid magic snaked over my skin, and I hugged myself under my cloak. The chanting was stirring something inside me, a magic old as death.

"Thanatos! Thanatos!"

At the sounds of their chants, a pit opened in my chest. His name—the true name of Death—rang in my skull.

"I don't think this is a good idea," I murmured to Ruadan.

"Why not?"

I could hardly breathe. "This magic is dangerous."

"Are you joking?" Acid laced his tone.

"Thanatos! Thanatos!"

How could I tell him the truth?

As the cultists chanted, dark magic blossomed in my body.

I will steal your food and your breath.

"Thanatos! Thanatos!"

I am the seeping darkness that bleeds over long grasses....

A strange tingling sensation shot down my shoulder blades, a power yearning to break free.

"Thanatos! Thanatos!"

I wanted to take to the skies, to unleash a magic that would ripple across the horizon like an atomic blast.

"Thanatos! Thanatos! Thanatos!"

I am the rot in your bones. I am the hunter, stalking you while you chatter.

Power simmered in me, responding to their chants. But I had to stay in control here. My fingernails pierced my palms so hard I nearly drew blood.

"Thanatos! Thanatos! Thanatos!"

Around us, the humans were chanting louder and louder, the rhythmic sounds stoking my blood to a fever pitch.

I am your final thought when the breath leaves your lungs. I am the sound of teeth hitting porcelain. I conquer all.

As they chanted, cold rage slid through my bones. Ruadan had begun carelessly unearthing everything I'd tried to bury.

"Thanatos! Thanatos!"

They were chanting his true name.

My father's true name.

I wanted to destroy it all.

As a child, I'd been a tomboy. Knees covered in mud and scrapes. When my pale, blond hair started darkening to a girlish lavender as I'd gotten older, I'd cut it short and covered it with a hat.

I am the tear in your heart, splitting open.

At the time, when Ruadan had invaded our world with his fae cohort, I'd looked very much like a boy. That simple fact was probably the only reason Ruadan hadn't tried to kill me yet. The only reason Ruadan hadn't already pieced it all together. Demigods—especially male demigods—were so damned sure of themselves.

He should die for his arrogance. He should kneel before me. They would all kneel before me in the end.

I am the rattle in your throat.

It had all been Ruadan's fault. If he'd never come, I'd be ignorant and happy. I'd still be there in the woods, baking pies with my mum, probably married off to some handsome fae bloke.

My gaze flicked to Ruadan's perfect features. The moonlight gilded the masculine planes of his face and sparked in his pale, violet eyes. He was the true destroyer, and a buried lust for vengeance stirred in me.

I could turn him purple, make his limbs rot. I could make the blood run from his beautiful lips.

When you're not looking, I enshroud you from the toes up.

My shoulder blades wanted to unleash my power.

Bow before me.

Ruadan's magic snaked over my skin, feeling strangely invasive. "What is wrong with you?" he whispered. "I can hear your heartbeat."

I whirled, my lip curling, rage carving through my belly like a knife.

I'm a creature who should never walk the earth. A monstrosity. An abomination. I'm on your kill list.

Ruadan had never seen my true monstrous side—nor I his. Would it come out now? Could I kill him before he killed me?

"Thanatos! Thanatos! Thanatos!"

The chanting grew louder, but my gaze was still locked on Ruadan, his on mine. Frigid wind swept past us, and the air seemed to darken around him.

He leaned in again, his pine scent surrounding me. His magic licked at my skin, slow and dangerous. "Blend in, Arianna." An unyielding command from the Grand Master.

Not my real name, demon. My real name is Liora.

The demonic general raised his hands to the night sky. "Without death, there is no pleasure!"

"Oh, great Lord Gamigin!" the crowd chanted in unison. "Without death, there is no pleasure!"

My heart was a wild beast. *Thanatos!* The chants roiled my blood.

Ruadan's eyes bored into me. "Get control of yourself," he said in a low voice. The shadows around him sucked in all the light.

I am death. I fought the impulse to clamp my hand around his throat and squeeze. "You need to stop messing with my mind." My voice sounded strange even to myself. "You don't know what you're toying with, demon. There are powers even you can't fight."

Night fell in his eyes, and he took a step closer, until I could feel his raw power thrumming over my skin. "You are here on a mission."

"And tonight," the demon boomed, "we celebrate pleasure!"

Out of the corner of my eye, I glimpsed shifting cloaks, skin bared in the moonlight. It was the first time I realized the crowd wasn't entirely made up of men. Women lurked among them, too—women who were opening up their cloaks, ready to celebrate pleasure with the men. Breasts and penises all over the place.

The sight was so startling and ridiculous that it snapped me right out of my spiraling death rage. The instinct I'd been fighting—to clamp my hand around Ruadan's throat—simply disappeared.

I took a deep breath. I had a bad feeling it would come back, but I was in the clear for now. They wouldn't get a death angel here tonight.

I stared as a woman leaned up against a wall, her back to her partner. He grabbed her hips from behind, hands running over her breasts.

Honestly. Some people.

What had Melusine said about the Great Mortality? Half the people were flogging themselves, the other half banging in the shrubs.

I guess we'd found the fun ones.

We were supposed to blend in, weren't we? I wasn't about to take off my cloak, but maybe we could look a little fun.

I took a step closer to Ruadan, then ran my hand up his chest. He stiffened. Then, I wrapped my arms around his neck and pressed my hips into him, my breasts brushing against him. I stood on my tiptoes.

Pure black had slammed into his irises, and he stared at me with an intensity that rivaled my own. He gripped my waist hard with one hand, the other sliding into my hair. Then, he whispered, "We've blended in long enough." Tension rippled off him, and he pulled away from me with what seemed to be a great deal of effort. "I'll trap Lord Gamigin. You question him."

At the head of the churchyard, the demon lord still chanted in Angelic.

I surveyed the revelers, the men and women writhing against each other. I couldn't say I was shocked to see Uncle Darrell standing in a corner on his own, desecrating a shrub. Of course he was here. If there was a public trouser-dropping opportunity to be had in the great city of London, Uncle Darrell would find it.

The Wraith took a step closer to Lord Gamigin, shadows billowing around him.

My fingers twitched. I really wanted to hurt the people working for Baleros.

The temperature around us plummeted, ice spreading over the ground and graves. My breath clouded in front of my face.

Just as Lord Gamigin's dark eyes landed on Ruadan, ropes of dark magic spun out from Ruadan's hands, snaking around the demonic lord.

The humans began screaming, already fleeing. With a dark smile curling my lips, I shadow-leapt over to Lord Gamigin and jumped down hard behind him. I whipped my iron knife from its sheath, and I plunged it into his shoulder blade.

He grunted with pain, trying to rip himself free of the magical constraints.

"You worship death, do you?" I began. "It could be your lucky night. A release from the torments of this world. Tonight, I saw my friend rip a man in two with just a flick of his wrist. Would you like that? Give your life a bit of meaning?"

"What do you want?" he grunted.

"I want to know where Baleros is," I said. "And Queen Macha."

His own magic was working against Ruadan's, but the iron in my dagger had already weakened him. "I don't know where Baleros is," he said through gritted teeth.

I pulled the dagger from his shoulder and held it to his throat, nicking the skin just a little. "You're one of his generals, aren't you?"

"I'm not telling you anything."

I pressed the blade in deeper. "You worship death because

you fear it. Tell me what I need to know, and I might let you live."

"I don't know where Baleros is. I'm the lowest-ranking general."

Godsdamn it. "Where do we find Queen Macha?"

He shook his head, his horns glinting in the moonlight. "I don't know."

"Tell me what you do know, demon, or I'll sacrifice you to Thanatos, since the goat didn't work out."

"I don't know where to find him, but there's a fae king. He of the fiery hair. He keeps Macha underground. Under the water."

Pressing the blade a little deeper, I demanded, "Where underground?"

"One of Baleros's generals, King Locrinus, is guarding Queen Macha. Beneath the wolf's grave. You'll never get to Locrinus. He's protected by the bean nighe and the Caoranach."

I had no idea what half of this meant.

The demon looked around, frantically. "But I will never tell his name. I'll die before I tell you his name!" he screamed valiantly into the skies.

"You already said Baleros's name, knob-end," I said. "What else do you know?"

"That's all we need," said Ruadan. "You might want to step away from the demon."

I jumped away from Lord Gamigin, and as I did, Ruadan's magic constricted, slicing through the demon's body. Just enough time for a final scream, then a gurgle. Ruadan had ripped him apart completely.

My lip curled. "I could have just used the knife. I honestly didn't know you had this brutal side."

Ruadan's back was already turned as he strode for the exit.

"Can you tell me where we're going?" I called out. "What's this about a wolf?"

"Whitechapel."

Jack the Ripper, hipster bars, imprisoned fae queens. Did anything good ever happen in Whitechapel?

My heart thumped in my chest like a war drum, and I stared at Ruadan, the man who'd destroyed my world, the one who wanted to kill me. My fingers twitched on my knife's hilt.

The day Ruadan had come into our world was the day everything had changed. We'd led a boring, domestic life, hidden in our own little realm with a small village of fae. We baked pies, played in the woods. I thought my dad was fae like the rest of us.

Then, my whole world had ended. My father—god of death—had killed everyone but me. How was it that he'd spared me? Was I so similar to him, a death angel myself?

I had a feeling Whitechapel's grim history wasn't about to get any rosier tonight.

CHAPTER 10

*O*ur footsteps echoed off the pavement as we moved north through the city. Nineteen hours till death hit the city.

Ruadan's fear magic was still with me, and my mind flashed with images of my mother's blood in the soil, droplets of crimson on the bluebells, red hair spread out—

"I can still hear your heart," said Ruadan.

His heart might not be racing, but he looked just as tense as I felt, each of his muscles taut, shadows seeping into the air around him.

I smiled sweetly. "How about I stop my heart from beating so it won't bother you?"

He shot me a sharp look.

"I don't suppose your heart ever beats too hard, does it?" I said. "You might as well not have one."

Ruadan, demigod of darkness, of icy control. So many things about him terrified me, and I couldn't bring myself to actually voice any of the thoughts in my head.

"What's bothering you?" he asked at last.

My heart sped up. *You've healed me. You destroyed my world.*

You've saved my life. You want to kill me. Someday, the truth will come out, and one of us will have to draw blood first. One of us will die. Someday, the truth will come out, and I'll have to face—

Nausea welled in my gut, and I hunched over, dry heaving. There was nothing left in my stomach, and I retched over the gutter. Eventually, I mumbled, "Until death us do part."

"What did you say?"

"I said, what's a wood-poppet? Is that a real thing?"

"No."

Ahhh. Ruadan's sense of humor, then. I wiped my mouth, hand shaking. "Your magic doesn't sit well with me. The spell you used back in the pub."

"Someday, you'll have to face yourself."

I froze in my tracks. "Please tell me you can't hear my thoughts."

"I can't. But I know guilt when I see it."

"I don't have anything to feel guilty about." I said it a little too sharply. I stood tall, staring him in the eyes. "Do you ever lose control, Ruadan, or have you been perfecting your icy resolve for seven hundred years? Has it ever cracked?"

"I'm half incubus. What do you think?"

"Boradrion said something about what happens when an incubus loses control." Incubi were rare. Apart from Ruadan and his half-brother, I'd never met any. "What happens then?"

Ruadan was already walking again, pulling his favorite "not answering" move.

I hurried after him. Scary as it would be, some part of me desperately wanted to see the incubus come out. The *real* Ruadan.

"How does it come about, your incubus side?" I asked. "What happens when it does?"

Baleros's first law of power: Get in your enemy's head. Knowledge gives you control over a person.

After another beat, he finally answered. "Fear brings it out, sometimes sex. My primal side takes over and it's hard for me to gain control again."

The way he answered so succinctly gave me the impression that he was answering with a mental bullet-point list rather than giving me insight into an ancient and terrifying psychological process. "Your primal side takes over?"

More silence, a thickening of shadows.

I couldn't imagine Ruadan often found himself afraid, but the impending Black Death certainly had him a bit rattled.

"So, do I need to know about what we're about to face underground?" I asked.

"When you saw King Locrinus in the hall, he was with a female. The one in the red dress made of human skin. That's the Caoranach."

"The serpent woman. I see. She and I had a little run-in down by The Spread Eagle."

"A run-in?"

"We tried to kill each other."

He stopped walking for a moment, then stared at me. The air thinned, a dangerous silence. "She tried to kill you, and you lived? How is that possible?"

Panic flickered through my thoughts. I'd lived only because of my death powers. Maybe no other creature could have withstood her.

"If she wanted to kill you," he added, walking again, "you'd have died. You and me both need to stay as far away from her as possible."

I bit my lip. "I didn't realize her dress was made of human skin."

"She lurks in underground rivers and transforms into a

serpent. She's four thousand years old. Some say she's not even fae."

"What is she, then?"

"One of the Old Gods, maybe. Grown from the earth itself. She drains her enemies, fills the rivers with their blood. She's loyal to anyone who will feed her with pain. King Locrinus does just that. But we can avoid her if we stay quiet. She's drawn by loud noises. As long as we're quiet, we can slip past her unnoticed."

"That might be a bit difficult." I frowned. I'd never met a bean nighe, but I knew mostly that they were demented washerwomen who screwed with your mind. "Am I right in thinking that bean nighe tend to scream?"

"Only if someone is about to die. Or if they want to alert the Caoranach, in which case people definitely die."

"So how do we avoid death, exactly? How do we stop them from screaming?" I frowned. "If the bean nighe scream, we die because the Caoranach comes for us. But they also scream *because* we're going to die…. I'm having a hard time working out the causal relationship when creatures can both predict and influence future events. Do you have any thoughts about this?"

"Cakes."

Leave it to Ruadan to cryptically answer a very complex question by just throwing out a random baked good with no other explanation.

"Did you just say *cakes?*"

"The bean nighe are fomoire. They feed off death and agony. But they also feed off cakes. And legend says, once you satiate them with cakes, they are forever in your debt."

"Are you messing with me again?"

"No."

I blinked. "I see. And you're carrying cakes on you, are you?"

"No." A gust of wind rippled over us, and he seemed to be done talking. After another moment, he added, "You are."

I frowned. "Have you been rifling through my bag?"

"I can smell the jam and sugar from here."

"Right." With any luck, these primordial harbingers of death could be bribed with a half a packet of Jaffa Cakes and the fondant fancy I'd picked up at Costcutter in lieu of feeding off our misery. "Well, hopefully they're not choosy."

CHAPTER 11

When we reached the Aldgate pump, Ruadan stopped walking. It was an old, derelict water fountain. A silver wolf's head gleamed over a grate in the pavement.

"What is this, exactly?"

"This is where the last wolf in the city of London died. The wolf's head marks the spot. Once, Londoners drank this water." Ruadan leaned over, pulling off the grate. "Until they realized the streams were fed by London's cemeteries, poisoning their water with diseases."

"So King Locrinus, Carver of Enemies, Ruler of Elfame, is hiding out in corpse-water. Charming. What happens after we bribe the bean nighe and slip past the Caoranach?"

He met my gaze. "We move silently—in the shadows. Our primary goal is to find Queen Macha. She's likely to have information that can lead us to Baleros. It's a rescue mission, not a kill mission." He gestured at the opened grate.

I leapt in first, splashing down in the dark water. The river nearly reached my knees, the cold water chilling me. Ruadan jumped down next, silent as he landed. He flicked his wrist, calling up a ball of dim silver light to illuminate our path.

I breathed in deeply, taking in a rich mineral scent in the air. It took me a moment to figure out that the chalky odor was calcium, and another second to put together that this smell came from human bones. Tonight's missions were taking us to London's grimmest locations, all those full of ancient bodies. I tried not to think about the bone particles rushing over my legs. I'd had enough of human bits this evening.

We moved deeper into the tunnel, water rushing around my calves. I moved as quietly as I could, acutely aware that any noises would draw the Caoranach.

As we moved in deeper, a heavier scent floated through the air—the smell of death.

Most people said the bean nighe were simple harbingers of death. If they screamed, you could bet someone was going to die, and that it would probably be you. But there was more to it than that. They stirred up your darkest thoughts before they killed you, and they fed off the pain.

Long ago, they had lingered unseen over childbirth beds, washing the rags of the dying women and babies, drinking up their agony. I imagined modern medicine had started to screw things up for them, but the world had more than enough pain to go around.

A mournful, keening voice wended through the tunnel. Then, over the melody, the frantic sound of a flapping bird's wings. The bean nighe's song wasn't the frantic screech that heralded death, but it set my teeth on edge anyway. Whatever the truth was about bean nighe, they tended to screw with people's minds, and my mind had taken about all the screwing it could take tonight.

I leaned in, grabbing Ruadan's arm to pull him down and whisper, "Can you do your little body-ripping trick?"

He shook his head, then whispered in my ear. "My powers don't work on fomoire."

"They don't? Why not?"

No answer, but he was still standing close to me, not pulling his head away.

My lip twitched. "I think I'm going to consider this our first date." So quiet I wasn't sure if he'd even heard it. We'd have a few dates in cemeteries and bone water, then we'd try to kill each other when the truth came out. A perfect relationship for me, really.

Instead of responding, he pulled away, walking silently through the water again. The truth was, even if I was angry at Ruadan, I wanted him so badly my ribs ached.

He'd ruined my life, and part of me still wanted more from him. Not just sex, but I wanted his secrets and his confidence and his trust. I wanted late-night conversations, my head resting on his chest to hear his heart, his arms encircling me. Gods help me, some part of me actually wanted to take *care* of this nightmarish demigod. I was on his kill list, and he'd told me relationships were forbidden anyway. Was I losing my mind completely? I sighed, a hollow opening in my chest.

As we walked forward, narrower tunnels branched off on either side of us, curving away into darkness. Escape routes if we needed them.

Ruadan sniffed the air, then turned to me. He placed a finger over his lips. I hadn't even been talking, and he wanted me to be quiet. The Caoranach was here.

Still, the bean nighe's singing grew louder, along with the rhythmic sound of beating of wings. I gritted my teeth, willing my heartbeat to slow. Ruadan flicked his wrist, and the ball of silver light brightened.

As we moved deeper into the tunnel, another pearly light glowed up ahead of us. In the gloom of a dank cemetery tunnel, a single bean nighe shone like the moon in the night. She wore a silver gown, black hair cascading over pale shoulders, and she scrubbed at a cloth. I hadn't expected the bean nighe to be so beautiful, and she drew me closer, like the moon drawing in the tides. A sheathed sword glinted on her back. I didn't suppose we could trade the cakes for their weapons as well?

From the shadows skulked two more armed bean nighe, their dark eyes wide. All three were singing, their voices mingling harmoniously, echoing off the tunnel walls. Each of them scrubbed a scrap of crimson cloth, and droplets of blood dripped into the river.

If three beautiful washerwomen didn't seem like much of a protective force, that was only because they hadn't launched into the real shit yet. Fortunately, we'd come armed with baked goods.

"Cakes," said Ruadan under his breath.

"I know what I'm doing," I mouthed.

I slid my backpack off my shoulders and reached for the Jaffa Cakes, shoving aside a change of clothes and a few crumpled Tube maps.

The bean nighe fell silent as we drew closer, eyes turning to us. They gripped their blood-soaked cloths.

I held out the Jaffa Cakes in front of me as we approached the closest woman. She cocked her head, eyes wide as she stared at the treat.

"Will you let us pass?" I whispered, pointing at the cakes. "If we give you these fine cakes, will you let us pass?"

The only response was that eerie sound of beating wings, like an invisible bird flapping all around us. The closest bean nighe cocked her head sharply—an eerie, reptilian movement.

I took a step closer. Maybe they hadn't heard me. "They're actually limited-edition *strawberry* Jaffa Cakes.

They're not the ordinary orange kind. They're quite… delectable."

A grin spread over her face. Despite the sharpened teeth she revealed, my shoulders began to relax.

The serving wench rolls an eighteen for her charisma check, and we are getting somewhere.

"If you let us pass, the Jaffa Cakes are yours." I shrugged. "I might even throw in a package of fondant fancies. Multicolored frosting. Unopened. Especially if we can borrow your swords for a bit."

Still grinning, the bean nighe nodded enthusiastically. Then, she dropped her bloodied cloth and snatched the box from my hand. The three washerwomen descended on the Jaffa Cakes, ripping them out of the cardboard and plastic, shoving them into their mouths. Crumbs rained down into the river.

When they finished, they ran their long tongues over their bony fingers, looking at me hopefully for more.

"You'll give me the swords, right?" I mouthed, pointing at their weapons.

All three nodded.

I reached into my bag, pulling out the fondant fancies—bright pink, yellow, and purple cakes, drizzled with chocolate. The bean nighe crowded around them, elbowing each other and snatching the cakes, mashing them into their mouths, grunting.

I crossed my arms, satisfied with my work. They'd agreed to the deal. They'd taken the cakes, and that meant our safe passage had been secured—swords and all. We'd already passed the first hurdle.

"Well," I whispered. "We'll just be on our way, then."

I took a step forward through the cold water, ready to brush past the three bean nighe.

As I did, the washerwomen dropped their glamour. They

transformed, hair whitening and growing tangled. Blood streamed from their eyes, and their singing rose to a keening fever pitch. The sight of their gaping, dark eyes hit me like a gale-force wind, knocking me back. What the hells?

The first bean nighe opened her mouth, and she shrieked, the otherworldly sound curdling my blood.

I clamped my hands over my ears, trying to block it out. Someone was about to die. But was it them or us?

CHAPTER 12

*S*o much for the legends about cakes.

I shot a glance at Ruadan, and he gave me a quick nod, which I interpreted to mean "kill them now." Gripping the knife, I began to rush forward, well aware that I'd brought a knife to a sword fight.

But as I moved forward, a wall of darkness slammed into my skull.

I stopped running and looked back at the clearing with a growing sense of horror. I stared at the red hair spread out over the soil, at the fae bodies rotting before us. My father stood over my mum, black wings swooping from his shoulders, his expression haunted.

He'd killed her. His wings of death had come out and disease had spread over the village. Fae wilted like flowers in the sun. I'd heard rumors of the Angel of Death. I'd never known he was my father.

I turned and ran again, desperate for the portal. I needed to put as much distance as I could between myself and the Angel of Death.

He'd killed everyone.

Hadn't he?

Fury exploded. I ripped myself free from the vision until I found myself in the tunnel again. As I'd been reliving my past, some primal part of my brain had taken over. Somehow, I'd managed to avoid the bean nighe's sword, shadowleaping around the tunnel.

I held my knife out in front of me, slashing it as a bean nighe moved closer. Her sharp teeth were bared, fury contorting her features. Swinging for her, battle fury blazed. I thrust the iron blade between her ribs, and her skin began to crumble and crack, the fissures of flesh weeping blood. *One down.*

Out of the corner of my eye, a flash of red hair.

Ruby's hair.

My heart leapt. I whirled. As I stared at the woman before me, the ground tilted beneath my feet.

Crimson cascaded over a white dress, eyes a pistachio green.

My chest tightened. "Mum?" I stammered.

Still alive. What's she doing here?

She reached for me. My legs shook, and I took another step closer, stretching out to touch her hand.

Ruadan shifted from the shadows and clamped his hand around my mum's head, snapping her neck. I felt the break as sharply as if it had been my own. Then, he tore her head off her body.

My screams echoed off the tunnel walls. A hollow opened in my stomach, and I blinked away the tears. "Why did you do that?"

He stared at me. "Why did I kill the bean nighe?"

I shook my head. Of course. I knew the bean nighe screwed with your mind. As I looked around me, I realized Ruadan had killed the other one, also. They were all dead.

"She looked like my mother," I muttered, before a jolt of

panic pierced me. Had I just given away my identity to Ruadan? Had he seen Ruby, too?

His violet eyes gleamed in the darkness. "That wasn't your mother. It was a bean nighe glamour, harvested from our own memories. She looked like someone else to me."

"Who?"

Darkness bled around him. "My wife."

I swallowed hard. "You said there was a legend about cakes. If we fed them cakes, they'd be in our debt."

"Legends aren't always accurate. If they were, we'd call them facts."

"Legends aren't always accurate," I repeated for emphasis.

Like the legend about how Adonis had created the Black Death. That one wasn't a fact, was it?

I gripped my knife, searching through the gloom for our next threat. "I don't understand. Did the bean nighe scream because *they* were going to die? It seems like a poor evolutionary trait, since the screaming caused their deaths…." My thoughts were getting tangled again.

Ruadan's attention was on the water below us. "Does it matter now?" He reached down, swiping his fingertips through the shallow river. The silver light from his orb illuminated blood dripping from his fingertips into the stream.

My bones chilled. All this blood wasn't just from the bean nighe—the river itself had turned to blood.

My gaze trailed up and down the underground river, and I could see nothing but blood all around us. This was the doing of the Caoranach, lured by the noise.

Ruadan snuffed out his light, and I felt a finger over my mouth, signaling silence. After another moment, I felt the hilt of a sword in my hand as he handed me one of the bean nighe's weapons. My muscles had frozen completely.

A rough, raspy sound carried through the tunnel, raising goosebumps on my skin.

Ruadan touched my cheek, then whispered, "Jump."

I clutched the lumen stone at my throat, summoning the cold, electrical magic.

I leapt—just as an explosion rocked the tunnel. Midair, I slammed into a hailstorm of oncoming rocks. Chunks of stone caught me in the shoulder and the hip, knocking me arse-backward into the blood river. I scrambled to my feet, gagging on the blood that had trickled into my mouth. Somehow, I'd managed to hold onto the sword.

From behind us, a snake's hiss rippled over the water. Ruadan hadn't been kidding. The Caoranach was bloody terrifying.

Ruadan grabbed me by the arm, pulling me up from the river. Then, he practically threw me into a tunnel that branched off the main one. In here, darkness consumed us completely.

"Jump," he said again—unnecessarily, since at this point I had very much internalized the concept of *run from the snake woman.*

Another loud explosion, and rocks rained down around us. How was she making these tunnels collapse? I blocked my head with my forearms as debris slammed onto my arms. I grunted with pain, falling to my knees and dropping my sword.

When the explosion had finished, I forced myself up again, grasping around until I found the sword. Ruadan reached for me, and he pulled me close against his powerful, damp chest. His muscled arm clamped around me, and I could hear the sound of his heart beating hard. I'd wanted to hear his heart. Just … not like this.

I wasn't sure where the Caoranach was now. Could she hear us if I asked him a question? My arms screamed where the rocks had slammed into them.

I stood on my tiptoes to get closer to Ruadan's ear, my body sliding against his. "How is she smashing the tunnels?"

His breath warmed my ear as he whispered. "Her tail. She's slipping around the tunnels, trapping us by collapsing walls."

I breathed in deeply. I hadn't understood exactly how *large* she could get.

Okay. So the great avoidance plan wasn't working. We'd have to kill the bitch.

Was it even possible to kill one of the Old Gods? Probably not, given that Ruadan was one of the most powerful creatures I'd ever met, and he was hiding in a hole to avoid her.

Down here, total darkness enveloped us, and the dank tunnel air felt oppressive. If it hadn't been for Ruadan's body warming mine through our wet clothing, I could almost imagine myself in the musty underground cage Baleros had kept me in. I'd grown used to being trapped underground, but being hunted by a snake woman was an unwelcome addition to the usual scenario.

Ruadan had said that she hunted through sound—especially loud noises. Right now, I could hear only his breath and mine. Was that enough to draw her closer?

As I pressed against Ruadan, her hissing grew louder, along with the raspy sound of scales rubbing against stone.

Shit, shit, shit.

Ruadan's arm loosened on me. I stepped away from him, tightening my fingers on the sword's hilt. The sound of my own breathing made my muscles tighten. I couldn't see a bloody thing in the damn tunnel. Ruadan, demigod of night, probably knew exactly what was going on, but it wasn't like he could tell me.

The coppery scent of blood grew stronger around us.

The Caoranach hissed again, and the sound slithered over my skin, raising bile in my throat. Then, when her body began to glow with faint golden light, all the breath left my lungs.

The serpentine lower half of her body practically filled the tunnel. She'd transformed into something different than she'd been before. Her face looked half-woman, half-monster: pale skin with two slitted nostrils; tiny, dark eyes and a wide mouth that showcased her fangs. Her eyes transfixed me, and I could hardly remember what I was supposed to do. Were we here to fight?

A dark, forked tongue flicked out of her mouth, and even in my mental fog, a survival instinct spurred me on to fight back. With a lightning-fast reflex, I slashed for her tongue. I cut into it just a little before she really hit me with it.

But before I could take another breath, she licked at us again. Ruadan swung for her, but her tongue hit his arm, then lashed at me. She caught me in the side, just below my ribs. I clutched the wound, already feeling the toxin spreading through me. The poison wound its way around my muscles, freezing me up. I dropped the sword into the blood river. Around me, the water was rising.

This was not a good situation. Ruadan and I were *both* about to be immobilized.

I gaped as the Caoranach transformed, her reptilian body contracting. No longer was there a giant serpent standing before us, but a woman clad in red leather, grinning at us. She had a tidy leather satchel at her waist—one that actually *did* look like it was made of human skin. I wanted to smash that grin right off her face.

Fear slid through my veins. I couldn't get out of this the same way I had before, not without potentially revealing my true nature in front of Ruadan. When he saw the death magic pulsing out of me, he might know. My blood roared in my ears. I willed my body to move. Still, I couldn't move a single muscle.

Ruadan had been hit, but he was still wielding his sword. He lunged forward, swinging for the Caoranach, but she dodged. Another lash from her tongue caught him in the side, and his body went still, a deep red gash showing through his clothing.

Panic began spiraling through me. The blood river was rising higher around us, at my waist now. Although I couldn't move my body of my own volition, my teeth chattered involuntarily.

When Ruadan dropped his sword into the rising blood, my stomach sank.

I could feel the ancient winds of death whispering through me.

Fae, demons, the unholy beasts who scrabble over the earth ... I will steal your breath.

Not my own voice. The voice of an Angelic horde, echoing off my skull.

The Caoranach smiled. "Now. Isn't this lovely? I have you both where I want you."

CHAPTER 13

*P*ale blue light from her body glowed over the
tunnel, gleaming over the rising river of blood. It
had reached my hipbones, now, the smell of blood overpowering.

The Caoranach began shivering, teeth chattering. Apparently, the cold bothered her, too, and Ruadan was delivering
heavy doses of ice. Frowning, she reached into her skin
satchel and pulled out a thermos, followed by a teacup.

With her talons clacking against the metallic thermos, she
unscrewed the top, then poured herself a cup of steaming
tea, one taloned pinky extended. She stared at us over the
rim of her teacup as she took a sip. Steam curled around her.

"Ahhhh…."

I hadn't admired her before, but now I had to admit the
woman was genius. I'd never thought to pack hot tea in my
bug-out bag. Assuming we got out of this situation, that was
the first thing on my agenda.

The Caoranach drifted closer to Ruadan, and she took
another sip of her tea. "I've been here since before the angels.

Before the fae. I am one of the Old Gods. Did you know that?"

Frozen in place, I caught a whiff of her tea. I didn't know what was in it, but it smelled like death.

She took another sip from her cup, the curls of steam winding around her head. "Mmmmm." She closed her eyes as she drank. "Do you know how I make this tea? I squeeze my victims to death, gut them, and then dry their organs. The agony they felt when I crush them continues to feed me after their lives have ended."

Gross. I still admired the thermos, but mine would not contain organ tea.

She knocked back the rest of her cup, then threw it against a wall. The porcelain shattered against the rock. Now, her body glowed even brighter with that pale blue light.

"You know me, Prince Ruadan. You remember me, don't you? I was there when you were just a young boy. I'm older than language," she went on, "and I will be here after all of your race dies. Demons. Fae. The lot of you."

With an iron will, I forced my eyes to move, to look at him.

The Caoranach was only inches from him now, her cheeks pink, eyes half-lidded. Her sights were locked on Ruadan, her expression starved. She carved one long, silver talon down his chest, ripping open his clothing.

"Can you stop making it so bloody cold?" she snapped.

Good luck with that, woman.

Ruadan looked like he was shifting—eyes darkening, the ghost of dark wings cascading down his back.

The temperature plummeted, the river growing so cold it was a shock to my body. My breath misted in front of my face. Immobilized, I shivered uncontrollably. Snake Lady shivered, too.

"I remember you, too, Prince Ruadan, demigod of the night," she hissed. "You were only a child when he brought you to me. You hadn't become powerful yet. Hadn't developed those fine muscles I see before me now."

So they *did* have a history. I'd thought as much when I'd first seen them together. No wonder Ruadan's rage was turning this place into the inner circle of hell.

An infuriating smile curled her lips, and she inched closer, sloshing through the blood. It was up to our ribs now, and freezing. "Your master, Baleros, used to feed you to me. Down in that bloody cave, just like this one. Do you remember how many times I froze you? And I cut your body?" She tutted. "Don't get so angry. It was all part of your training. It made you strong, didn't it? Look at the man you are today. And it was such a wonderfully delicious sustenance for me. Your pain was finer than that tea."

My stomach twisted. She'd been his torturer.

He couldn't move, but I felt his primordial magic snaking over me all the same.

The World Key glowed on his bared chest—a stunning gold among all the gloom. But Ruadan didn't quite look like himself anymore. His skin had taken on a silvery hue, and phantom wings swept out behind him. And as his skin changed, it looked as if he were pushing the toxins out of his body. She didn't seem to notice. What would happen if he shifted fully? I was starting to think we might have a chance, here, even without my death powers.

The Caoranach slashed a talon across his chest, and blood poured from the wound. "Baleros feeds me. He always has. The least I could do is give him this little bit of skin from your chest." Her gaze flicked to me. "Has she told you what she really is, yet? She's not fully fae. Anyone can tell that. So what sort of demon is she? A demigod like you?"

My mind screamed. I didn't want to dwell on this particular topic.

She hugged herself, shivering. "I don't like the cold."

Her tongue shot out again—this time, stroking up his body. She didn't break the skin. Rather, the movement was distinctly sexual. Rage erupted inside me.

My angelic side was threatening to come out to play, but if I unleashed the terror of the gods, my secret would be known.

"A demigod," she purred, a taloned hand groping his chest. Her lips had turned blue, teeth chattering. Ice formed around her body. "What a wonderful gift Baleros had given me. You can come so close to death. I could torment you to the point that your mind would break over and over again. But you never died. Such a wonderful … gift…." Her teeth were now chattering so hard she could hardly form words, and her eyes lost focus.

At that moment, Ruadan roared. He gripped her neck and twisted, the snap of bone echoing off the walls.

But she wasn't dead yet. With her neck disturbingly crooked, the lower half of her body began shifting. A scaled tail erupted from where her legs had been. Her serpentine form filled the tunnel, tail thrashing. Ruadan reached down into the rising blood and snatched his sword. He swung for her, hacking into her bent neck. Her shrieks pierced the air. Her body thrashed, tail booming against the tunnel walls as he cut off her head.

Except her tail just kept going on its own.

Light debris rained down on us, and I desperately wished I could cover my head with my arms to shield my skull.

Ruadan turned to me, his skin an eerie silver. How exactly had he broken free—just his sheer demigod strength?

I didn't have much time to contemplate it. The walls around us were shaking, and so was my body.

With Ruadan's rage freezing the air, the blood river chilled me to the marrow, and chunks of ice floated around us. Great mounds of rubble blocked our paths.

Ruadan lifted me into his arms, then carried me up to the top of the rubble. With his warm body pressed against me, I tried moving a muscle. I managed just one tiny movement—a twitching of my pinky finger as we reached the top of the rubble. That was it.

Holding me tightly, he carried my frozen body down the rubble on the other side.

The walls boomed again, large chunks of rock raining down around us. We were going to be buried alive in here, entombed by that creature's disembodied tail. As we plunged back into the river, the blood froze my body, rising higher, up to my breasts. Ice crystallized around us.

The loudest boom of all, and my heart slammed against my ribs. Ruadan pulled me tighter against him.

I clamped my eyes shut and braced myself for the collapse of the walls around us, for rocks battering my flesh, slamming into my skull—but I felt only Ruadan's powerful arms around me, his breath on my neck. Why hadn't the rocks slammed down on us?

I looked up at Ruadan's eyes, but I found only darkness. But behind his shoulders, a glimmer of starlight.

What in the hells…?

It took me a moment to realize what had protected us from the debris. Ruadan had unveiled his incubus wings, and they spread above us like a shield. The black, leathery wings gleamed with silver flecks like tiny stars. Faint light beamed from them over my skin and glinted off the icy blood river.

Right now, Ruadan had gone into his primal mode. Was this it? Was this him fully shifted? And if so—was this a bad situation?

His primal side had taken over, and I could barely move.

Not to mention the fact that I was close to freezing to death, and Ruadan didn't seem to be able to control his ice rage. The only mercy at this point was that the blood river seemed to be receding.

Still, I was pretty sure that the way he'd spread out his wings, he was protecting me. Even in his demonic form, he was shielding me.

"Ruadan," I tried to whisper, but my muscles still wouldn't move the way I wanted them to. My teeth were chattering so hard I thought I might involuntarily bite my own tongue off.

He cocked his head, the movement pure animal. A low growl rumbled from his throat, trembling through my gut. Right now, I was completely reliant on Ruadan. But was the fae I'd come to know in there at all? Or was this some hellish demon from the shadow void, about to tear my throat out if I annoyed him?

His dark, preternatural gaze trailed over my damp chest, then he lowered his head to my throat. One powerful arm held me close to his hard body. Right now, I had a hard time reconciling this creature with the controlled, distant fae who ran the Institute.

He opened his mouth, and my pulse began racing out of control. His canines had lengthened completely. In fact, they looked like vampiric fangs….

His fingers clutched my waist so hard I was certain he was going to leave marks. I stared into his dark eyes. This wasn't the Ruadan I knew, but a bestial creature of the void. And right now, he seemed fixated on my throat.

My heart beat harder, and I fought to move my lips, my vocal chords. My attempt to say his name only came out as a moan. Godsdamn it, I wanted to move. How had *he* managed to break free?

Powerful shivers wracked my body again. Ruadan unleashed a long, slow growl, his dark magic snaking over my skin. His hard body pressed against me, warming me. My neck arched, and his eyes were locked on the vein in my neck, the pulsing blood. His tightly coiled muscles gave the impression of an animal about to strike. My heart pounded like a drum.

Incubi didn't drink blood. Did they?

Then, to my horror, he moved. His fangs pierced my throat—a sharp, delicious pain.

CHAPTER 14

*E*cstasy bloomed in my body. Ruadan's tongue flicked against my skin, and my mind burst with images of the night sky, like an explosion of stars. My eyes fluttered closed, and I melted into him, muscles softening. My toes curled with white-hot pleasure, and I moaned. I'd never let anything bite me before.

No, no, no. Was he going to drain me? Was he even in there, under the demonic exterior? What the fuck was going on?

"Ruadan," I groaned. It took me a moment to realize that this time, I could say his name.

My fingers twitched, then my arm. I moved my hips a little, brushing against Ruadan's warm body—which seemed to have become even larger.

Ruadan pulled his mouth from my neck, and I reached up to touch his face.

I could move again. I blinked up at him. How had that happened?

He licked a droplet of blood off his fangs.

I ran my tongue over my lips, finding that I had control

over my mouth once more. Now, the river's surface had lowered, back down to my hips once more.

Ruadan was still holding on tightly to me, and I slid my arms around his neck.

"Did you suck the toxins out of my blood on purpose?"

"Why else would I be sucking blood from your neck?" His voice sounded different—deeper, and otherworldly. In his clipped tones, I had the sense of barely restrained anger.

"Why would you be sucking my blood? Because you've fully transformed into a terrifying demon with giant leathery wings. With stars embedded in them." I reached up and touched his wing, running my fingertips over the apex.

He shuddered, and each one of his muscles tensed. He gripped me so hard now that it started to become painful. "I'm not fully transformed," he said. The tips of his claws pierced my skin.

Wait.

"You have claws?" The chattering of my teeth echoed in the small space. "Never mind. How did you free yourself from that woman's toxins? And how were you able to suck them out of my throat without poisoning yourself?"

"She imprisoned me for decades, feeding off me. I built up a tolerance to her toxins. I never let her know."

I stroked the side of his face. I wanted to wrap him up and keep him warm by a fireplace forever. "Can we get out of here? The blood river is full of ice. I'm about to freeze to death."

Ruadan flexed his wings, and rock rained down from them. Apart from the silver flecks in his wings, almost total darkness enshrouded us.

He straightened, finally releasing me. I surveyed the dim space, lit only by the faint light from Ruadan's wings.

The wall of debris blocked one side of the tunnel—the side we'd just come from. Dust clouded the air, and I coughed. "I guess we have nowhere to go but forward," I said.

I desperately wanted out of here. When Ruadan created another ball of silver light, I looked down at the river again. The blood was gone, and clear water rushed around us. The Caoranach, it seemed, had left us.

Still, red streaked my white dress, and my lip curled in disgust. "Godsdamn it, Ruadan. Can you turn off the ice?"

He ignored me, plowing on. I had the sense he didn't have much control over the temperature, and in his partially shifted form, he certainly had no desire to explain it.

After a few minutes, we came to another pile of rubble, and it nearly reached the ceiling. At the base of the rubble, Ruadan turned to me, his features cold as marble. Then, he lunged forward and grabbed me around the ribs. He hoisted me up as if I weighed nothing, dropping me farther up the pile. His partially shifted incubus side was irritatingly dominating.

"I can move on my own," I snapped through chattering teeth.

Truthfully, although Ruadan had sucked the toxins out of me, my body still wasn't working as it should. It felt as if ice had flooded my own blood, and every one of my muscles had gone rigid. As I climbed up the rocks, I was shivering out of control.

At the top of the rubble, we had only a few feet of space to crawl through, and it seemed to go on for a few yards. Walls had collapsed around us, and darkness yawned on either side, but most of the ceiling remained intact. As I crawled through the gap, the broken stone bit into my palms and my knees.

When I reached the end of the gap, the broken rock sloped downward into the river. Here, the water smelled clear, and it was only about a foot deep. As we reached the bottom of the rubble, the silver flecks on Ruadan's wings illuminated the dark water.

Up ahead, a beam of moonlight streamed into the tunnel, pouring in from a grate or something above. I hugged myself as I walked through the cold water. At this point, I'd mostly gone numb.

I breathed in again, taking in a floral scent. In the dim light, it took me a moment to realize there were vines growing on the walls down here, all of them flowering with white blossoms. Moonflowers, in fact. I hadn't expected to find beauty down in the sewers, but here it was. As Ruadan walked past the flowers, frost spread over their leaves, and the petals crystallized with ice. The moody bastard was killing everything.

"Ruadan," I said sharply. "Stop it with the damned ice. She really got to you, didn't she? She used to feed off your pain. She tortured you, and she's a monster. But you're the one who told me to master my emotions."

He whirled around, his expression unreadable.

I understood, even without him explaining. Baleros had sacrificed a young fae to that tea-drinking, skin-flaying monster.

I stepped closer to Ruadan. "I know how it would have happened. Baleros would have told you that he was doing you a favor. He was making you strong, you see. He was making you into a powerful warrior. But he had an ulterior motive. He wanted to curry favor with one of the Old Gods, and so you were a sacrificial victim. He'd torture you while convincing you he had your best interests in mind."

Violet magic sparked up and down his body, glinting off the edge of his wings. *That* was his incubus lust magic, but he was keeping it contained. He was protecting himself. Just a stony expression, eyes black as night. It seemed like his incubus form protected him so that he didn't have to feel anything. All his emotions were on the outside, making the air cold. With his wings out, claws sharpened, nothing could hurt him.

The survivor in me told me I had to do the same in my own way, that I had to protect myself. If I got close to him, if I let myself care for him, I wasn't sure I could take it when he learned the truth about me. I couldn't let myself love him and then watch darkness slam into his eyes when he realized who I really was.

The betrayal would kill me before the sword ever did.

Still, I needed him to get control of his emotions right now, or I'd freeze to death. I had the strange sense that if he could say it out loud, it might help. I moved closer to him, until I was within touching distance. His transformed appearance sent shudders through my bones, but he trans-fixed me all the same. Shadows bloomed around him—a miasma of darkness. His face betrayed nothing, his beautiful features like cold marble.

I pressed my palm flat against his cheek, trying to warm him. I held his gaze steadily. "What did she do to you? What did she and Baleros do?"

I brushed my thumb over his cheek, softly, and a chink of light flickered in his dark eyes.

He stared at me for what seemed like ages. At last, he spoke. "When I was a child, she kept me in a river of blood. Severity is the way of the Shadow Fae of Emain. It's how we grow strong. But her ways were extreme even for us. She carved my flesh from my bones, over and over. She'd bring me near death and feed off the torment. She grew strong off me."

Rage shot through me, hot and red. I'd save it for Baleros —this pure destruction trapped inside me. I'd keep it locked in my chest until it was time to unleash its full force.

"I cannot die," Ruadan went on in his emotionless voice.

"At least, she could not kill me. Few know how to kill a demigod. It was as you said. Baleros told me the torture would make me stronger. It was part of my training. I was in and out of there for years until I reached adulthood. And then, I was of age. I was married. I was free."

I pulled my hand from his cheek. Impulsively, I reached out and stroked the top of his wing, and his sharp intake of breath echoed off the walls.

"Baleros was lying to us when he told us he'd make us strong," I said. "But here's what he never envisioned: that we *would* become strong, and we would come for him."

Ruadan's dark eyes surveyed me. Blood from the river streaked his bare chest. We'd gone right into his worst memories—the river of blood, the Caoranach. We'd practically relived it. No wonder he hated being trapped in places.

"I'm getting this blood off you," I declared. "I know you think you don't care right now, because you're an incubus and you don't feel normal emotions, but it will help to bring the real Ruadan back. Then maybe you can ease up on all the ice."

I reached down to the freezing river and scooped up the clear water, then splashed it over his chest. He stared down at me, unmoving. As I washed off his skin, violet magic pulsed from his body over mine.

Did he realize he was dosing me with little waves of his lust magic? As I cleaned the blood off him, a shiver of pleasure washed over me, and my skin heated. Being this close to Ruadan in his incubus state was a dangerous game, one that made my breasts feel tight against my damp dress. He stared down at me, impassive, and another wave of his magic rippled over my body.

This was very dangerous territory indeed.

CHAPTER 15

I brushed his bare skin with my fingertips, licking my lips. Water mixed with blood, turning pink. "There," I said, my voice husky. "You'll feel better."

Till death us do part. I shoved the phrase out of my mind, and I watched the rivulets of pink streaming off him. Breath clouded around my face.

For some reason, I'd expected that, once cleaned of blood, he'd return to his usual form. Instead, he still loomed over me, wings spread. Not Ruadan anymore—just an ancient predator, looking at me like I was prey. A low, slow growl rose from his chest, rippling over my body. What exactly was happening?

Chunks of ice floated around my legs, and I was pretty sure my lips and skin had turned blue at this point. As much as I wanted to feel the warmth of his body, I took a step away from him, suddenly unsure of myself.

Ruadan cocked his head, gaze sweeping over me. Then, a glimmer of violet returned to his dark eyes. "You're freezing," he said. The dark wings behind him had started to fade— only phantom wings once more.

"Yes, thank you." I threw my hands up. "I've said that repeatedly for the past twenty minutes."

He reached for me, then pulled me close to his hard body. His warmth caressed my skin, and I leaned into him. My muscles began to relax. His body crackled with violet light, his magic warming me from the inside out. Still, I couldn't linger too long against him. I couldn't keep letting myself feel close to someone who was clearly my enemy.

A powerful hand stroked up my spine, and the air around us began warming. I started to forget about the whole enemy thing as my pulse began racing.

The water around us, too, began warming, ice melting. I met Ruadan's gaze, and he looked down at me, then gripped the top of my stained dress.

"Blood." A simple statement of fact, but his hand was gripping my dress so hard that the fabric cut into my skin. Frost tinged the air once more, and his wings spread out behind him—thick and gleaming with silver chinks.

I'd been right. The blood had bothered him. It reminded him of *her.*

With a great deal of force, I pulled his hand from my dress. "Calm down. I'll get it off me."

I had another dress stuffed into my bug-out bag. I slipped the bag off my shoulder, then I crossed to one of the walls. I hung the bag from a jagged outcrop.

I looked down at my dress, feeling uncharacteristically self-conscious. There was something about unbuttoning the dress in front of Ruadan that felt like a sensual performance. My cheeks heated as I undid the top, exposing my bra. Normally I'd just tear the thing off and toss it away, leaving the other person to process the awkwardness of my nudity. But this felt different, the air so charged that I couldn't meet his gaze. I couldn't even think about touching him or I was sure he'd pick up on my desire.

I could feel his eyes on me—Incubus Ruadan did not look away from bared skin. I wanted him to see me, all of me. At the same time, I felt like if I looked up at him, the world would combust.

I unbuttoned it down to my navel, and a raw, sexual energy skimmed and buzzed over my chest. My breasts seemed to strain against my bra, nipples peaking. Still, I kept my eyes down, just feeling the charge of his gaze stroking over every inch of my naked skin. Goosebumps rose on my bare flesh, and I unbuttoned the dress down to my hips.

My chest flushed, and at last, I dared to look up at him just a little, only raising my eyes as high as his torso. His body looked taught, tightly coiled. His violet magic crackled in the air, and lust pulsed across my naked skin.

He took a step closer, and my eyes swept over his muscled chest. His magic licked at my skin, warming me in places I badly wanted to feel him, a silky touch that heated my neck, my breasts, between my legs…. Molten heat swept through my core. I was wildly turned on, and Incubus Ruadan was feeding from my desire. Fueling it, too.

At last, I looked all the way up into his eyes, and blazing lust lit me up.

I unbuttoned the final button. The dress fell away, and I stood before him in my black bra and knickers, my pulse racing out of control. A muscle twitched in his jaw, his eyes black as the void again.

Violet-tinged light flickered around him, and my body ached for him. His attention was on me and me alone.

The corner of my lip twitched in a seductive smile.

That was all it took for him to move for me—a blur of black and violet, and he dropped all his restraint. He grasped me, pushing me against a wall, and the stone bit into my back. His powerful body pressed into me. I gasped, my legs opening wider. My neck arched, and I stared up at him. His muscled body pressed hard against me, and his eyes seared me.

He leaned down to kiss me. After the rough start, I expected something desperate, animal. But he was holding back. His lips moved sensually over mine—surprisingly gentle, stroking mine. I swept in my tongue, deepening the kiss, and he responded to it. His hands gripped my bare waist, then moved up my ribs, the pressure from his powerful fingers leaving a trail of heat on my body.

He pulled away from the kiss, and I nearly moaned. Then, his mouth moved over my neck, leaving a trail of searing hot kisses. My entire world right now was just his mouth, his hands, his heat. He caressed my body as he kissed me, until his thumbs traced the hollows of my hipbones, dipping under the hem of my knickers.

I moved my hips closer to him, encouraging his touch. His thumbs slid down further, skimming my skin and teasing me until, at last, one of his thumbs swept gently between my legs, the touch so painfully light I wanted to scream. I grasped his face in my hands, kissing him urgently, demanding that he move faster, harder. Another devastatingly light sweep of his thumb, and I groaned, moving harder against him, grinding myself onto his hand. I wanted him to let go completely.

I wrapped my arms around him, pulling him closer, and his kiss grew wilder with uncontrolled need. Then, his restraint seemed to snap. With a low snarl, he drew a long, silvery claw through the center of my bra, ripping it open. The tip of his nail grazed my skin, and the black lace fell away, revealing my breasts.

He kissed me again, claws just barely piercing my skin until I felt their sharp points retract. I writhed against him. As he kissed me—hard, this time—I moaned into his mouth, my body pure fire. I needed more from him, and the hot ache between my legs was driving me mad. My bare skin brushed against his, smooth and hot. I thrust my hips closer to him, nipples brushing his chest. I felt like I'd never get enough of him, and I needed him inside me now.

His hand slid down my back, firm pressure and hot skin, until it dipped into the back of my silky knickers. His touch singed me. I gasped, breath coming faster. I ached for him. Liquid fire flowed through me as he slid down my panties, and the tunnel air whispered over my naked skin.

For just a moment, I pushed him away. I wanted him to look at me—really look at me.

His slow, predatory gaze swept up and down my body— moving down past my breasts, my belly, lingering between my legs, the intent gaze of a hunter…. This time, I didn't lower my eyes. His magic lashed the air around him, and the power of his eyes on me ignited me. Dark wings swept behind him. A god of darkness, laser-focused on me.

Then, I reached for him, grabbing him by the waist of his trousers. I pulled them down, and within moments, he was lifting me up against the wall, hands gripping my bum. I wrapped my legs around him and thrust my fingers into his hair.

He whispered my name, his breath warming the side of my face. He was bringing out the wild beast in me, and I raked my fingertips down the front of his chest. He released a low growl. When he claimed my mouth, his kiss had grown savage. Both of us had lost all sense of restraint. He slid between my thighs, filling me. I felt my teeth on his neck, tasted the salt on his skin, and I groaned.

* * *

WITH MY LEGS still wrapped around Ruadan, I leaned into him, and the scent of pine enveloped me. I breathed deeply.

It took me a moment to realize that his wings had disappeared completely.

I cupped my hand against the side of his face. Now, the air felt warm—humid, almost. "The incubus is gone."

This was the real Ruadan. Unfortunately, this was also the Ruadan who wanted to kill me.

All at once, the horror of that thought slammed into my skull. I disentangled my body from his, sliding down his naked skin into the cold water once more. I didn't look him in the eye as I reached for my bug-out bag.

I tuned out the fact that Ruadan was saying my name, and I kept my gaze down. I pulled out my spare knickers and a simple black dress.

"Arianna," he said again.

That's not my name. My name is Liora.

Who would win in a fight between us? My father—the Angel of Death—hadn't been able to kill him. I had to think tactically, here, if I didn't want to die.

I tried to keep the tremor out of my voice as I asked, "How can Baleros kill you if you're immortal? You said almost no one knows how to kill demigods." I turned my back to him as I slipped on the new pair of knickers, like we were strangers again.

"There are two ways to kill a demigod," he said, his velvety voice rumbling over my skin. "One involves an Angelic spell—"

"Stop." I whirled and moved for him, covering his mouth with my hand. "I don't want to know."

The survivor in me was doing a shitty job right now. Maybe it was because I still wanted to feel Ruadan holding me close to his body, his heart beating against me.

"I've heard you speak Angelic," he murmured. "I'm not worried."

He had a point. My language abilities were nearly nonexistent, even if Angelic was my father's native language.

He kissed my cheek, so softly that I ached for him anew. "Are you worried you might lose your temper and slaughter me some day?"

Basically, yes. That was exactly what I was worried about.

I took a deep breath, not meeting his eyes. I pulled away from him, my body suddenly cold in his absence. "Look, what we just did was obviously a mistake. You said no lovers at the Institute, and that's a good idea. We're supposed to be working together, right? Let's not let it happen again, okay?"

As soon as the words were out of my mouth, ice frosted the air again.

I dared to look at him, and for just a brief, horrible moment I caught a glimmer of a wounded look. Then, his gaze shuttered again, and he fell silent. Ice skimmed over the river.

Emptiness yawned between my ribs, and I gritted my teeth, eager to change the subject. I stepped over a jagged bit of rubble. "Any idea where we're going?"

He sniffed the air. "Wyverns."

CHAPTER 16

"What, now?" I said. "Wyverns?"

"I smell them. We need to move in their direction. They're used as guards."

I breathed in deeply, scenting the air. A musky scent hit my nose, tinged with cedar embers. I'd never seen one of the reptilian creatures. I only knew they were enormous and muscular, and they breathed fire. "So that's what a wyvern smells like. Always wondered." I tried to keep my voice steady and light, forcing myself to ignore the dark truth that followed behind us like a stalker—that Ruadan and I were fated to be enemies.

Still, my voice came out sounding unnatural. I had no doubt that Ruadan had noticed. He noticed everything—my heart beating faster, my cheeks reddening. A man who saw everything and betrayed nothing.

"You think they're guarding Queen Macha?" I asked. And there was that unsteady tone in my voice again.

"Yes. Once we find her, we can use a portal to get out of there."

Unfortunately, we couldn't use a portal to get in without knowing where, exactly, she was.

Silence fell, broken only by the sound of our legs sloshing through the icy water. Our passionate moment had been just a temporary thaw, but as soon as I'd told him it was a mistake, we were back to wintry temperatures.

Still, I'd done the right thing by putting a stop to it, hadn't I? I was too much of a survivor to rush headfirst into something that would kill me.

Now, the silence felt worse than before—sharp and dangerous. I let out a long, slow breath.

Where was my life headed, exactly? I couldn't stick around the Institute forever—not while I was on Ruadan's kill list. But I couldn't quite bring myself to leave, either. Not yet. Bizarrely, the Institute was starting to feel like my home.

I had to say something to Ruadan, to smooth things over and to warm the place up again. Something that would probably start with, *About what just happened....*

But instead, I cleared my throat, my blood roaring. "Wyverns smell like musk. Bit like an old man's cologne."

Nope. That was not what I'd been going for.

"I, um…." I tried again. "The thing is…. Did you know that palm trees are actually a type of grass?"

Shit. Turned out, I was terrible at relationship talks.

Ruadan's eyes stayed straight ahead, his mouth closed in a firm line.

"How are we going to fight the wyverns, anyway?" I went on.

"Stab them through their eyes, pierce their brains."

I nodded at his sword. "We only have one of those, I notice."

He handed it to me, and I gripped the hilt tightly. It was a relief to have a proper weapon in my hand. Now, I could think about killing instead of the deeply uncomfortable topic of emotions.

As we reached a fork in the tunnels, the scent of musk grew overpowering. A low growl reverberated through the stony passages. I held my breath as we turned a corner.

The tunnel opened up into an enormous cave of turquoise water, its surface glimmering under Ruadan's silver light.

"How long can you hold your breath?" asked Ruadan.

"I guess we'll find out." I frowned. "You think your mother is being held below the water?"

"I can smell the wyverns all over the walls here." His gaze flicked upward at the enclosed ceiling. "And there's no other way out."

"And your mother can breathe underwater?"

"No. There must be a watertight chamber down there. We just have to get to it."

Ruadan dove under the surface, and his silver orb plunged into the water after him. I took a minute to suck in a long breath, filling my lungs. Then, I went in after him, kicking my legs hard to catch up. As I swam, the sword felt heavy in my hand, slowing me down a little.

Ruadan's sphere cast a dull, pearly light in the water. My lungs felt heavier the deeper we went, and after about thirty seconds, I started fantasizing about air. Sweet, sweet air in my lungs. It seemed to be endless turquoise water down here, tinged with the silver streaks of light.

Air.

Gods below, please don't make me endure the humilia-tion of having to give in and swim up for air.

At last, the silver light glowed over contours—something concrete lay before us. Rough stone, stairs…. A palace of sorts?

My lungs burned, but I focused on the structure taking

shape before me. Ruadan's sphere of light grew brighter, another floating high above. They casting silver light over a rough, crumbling stone staircase, and an archway with a tower that rose into the dark waters above. The stern, carved face of a river god glowered from the tower, and carvings of octopus arms snaked over imposing columns. A marble man stood with his arms outstretched to the river's surface, as if worshiping the air above…. *Air. Sweet, sweet air.*

Maybe I couldn't die, but I sure as shit could feel pain.

What the hells was this place? I was starting to feel light-headed, and I focused on tightening my grip on my sword's hilt. If I dropped my weapon, it'd all be over.

I'd been in many dangerous situations before, often with the odds stacked against me. But an underwater fight with giant reptiles was a bit beyond even my skillset. I could only hope the fight would happen once we breached the airtight chamber, and not while I was about to pass out under icy water.

I started to grow frantic for a breath, and I kicked my legs faster, now, urging Ruadan to increase his pace with me.

I mentally made a note that, in addition to a thermos of tea, my bug-out bag needed scuba-diving equipment.

We swam through the archway, then followed the trail of crumbling stairs up to an open door to the temple. Ruadan pushed on the door, and it shifted over a stone floor. His pale hair floated in the water around him. He squeezed inside the door, and I went in after him into a hall.

Statues with broken arms lined either side of us, their eyes gaping, noses missing. My throat was starting to spasm, now. What would happen if I drowned down here? Would my father bring me back to life again this time?

And how many times could I die in front of Ruadan before he pieced it all together? That little boy had been a girl

—one who'd escaped, and who'd grown into a woman with purple hair.

A burst of fire shot out in the murky water, startling me.

Ah. We'd reached a wyvern—and, unfortunately, I still hadn't reached the air.

My heart stuttered as the enormous creature swam out from behind a corner. The wyvern's scales shone in the dull underwater light, and it opened its mouth to breathe fire. A small burst of flames shot from its mouth, dulled by the cold water. I swam closer, sword ready. Ruadan reached him first.

Ruadan reared his fist back, then punched it hard into the creature's eye. With his arm thrust into the wyvern's head, he jerked it around a bit. I stared as he gripped hard onto what I could only imagine was the wyvern's brain. The wyvern's scream floated through the water, and a dull flame burst out of its mouth before dying out again. The sight of Ruadan hand-lobotomizing the wyvern had been so gruesome, I nearly forgot about the oppressive pain in my lungs. Blood spilled into the water around them, snaking through the darkness.

Good. That's over.

No sooner had the thought crossed my mind than a hot blast seared my back, and I whirled to find another wyvern behind me. At this point, darkness was swirling in my mind, but my survival instincts began to take over.

The thing lunged for me, jaw opened. I thrust my sword at its eye, but with the friction underwater—not to mention the oxygen deprivation— the movement was off. The wyvern snapped for my arm, sinking its sharp teeth into my skin. Blood stained the turquoise water.

Darkness bloomed in my lungs, a sharp pain that threatened to eat me alive from the inside out. My throat spasmed. *Air. Air. Air.*

The wyvern tore at my arm.

I am the twilight shadow that creeps over long grasses....

The death angel in me was taking over. I just couldn't let it take over completely—couldn't let the real Liora come out.

I am the hunter who sneaks up behind you when you're trying to find the right words. I stalk in your shadows as you search to fill the silence, skirting away from the dark truth.

No—not now. My heart was a hunted animal.

I tried to shove the death instinct deeper inside of myself. I needed Arianna to fight this battle. Not Liora.

When you look away, I enshroud your body, creeping up from your feet to claim your life.

I knew how it would end. Ruadan would see what I really was, and he'd come for me. The betrayal would take the fight out of me.

Something tingled at my back, a hot rush where wings might grow.

No!

I had to finish this without shifting here.

With one final act of iron will, I forced the death instinct under the surface, and I thrust my sword into the wyvern's eye. Clouds of blood bloomed around us. I twisted it sharply, and the wyvern's body spasmed and twitched.

If I didn't take a breath within the next few seconds, the death angel would come out for good, and it would all be over.

CHAPTER 17

I whirled, catching a glimpse of Ruadan slaughtering another wyvern with his bare hands. Blood muddied the water around him. He pulled his arm out of the wyvern's head, then turned to look at me.

Through the flash of panic in his eyes, I had a hint of how I must look to him. I hadn't transformed into my angel form, but blood flowed from my arm, pooling in the water around it—red tendrils, curling around me like ribbons. I was certain my eyes were bulging, and the look of sheer terror on my face was probably unnerving.

He moved for me, a blur of black through the water. In the next moment, his mouth was on mine. I opened my lips, and he breathed into my lungs.

Air, thank the gods.

I don't think I'd ever loved him more than I did at that moment.

I turned from him, and I frantically searched the space around us for a way in. There didn't seem to be any doors….

It took me a moment before I spotted the entrance just above us—a hatch with a wheel, embedded in the top of the arch. And that was our way into a tower that hopefully contained a whole lot of air.

My lungs seared me from the inside out. I gripped the metal and began turning the wheel with all the strength I had left. At last, the hatch opened, a stone door sliding to the side. Desperate, I hoisted myself up into a dark chamber, and I sucked in a deep, glorious breath as soon as my head breached the surface. I flopped over onto a stone floor. Ruadan came in after me.

His silver sphere bobbed in the air above us, illuminating broken statues that jutted from the towering walls. I gasped for breath and surveyed the space around us. Stony rib vaults arched high above us, like a medieval cathedral. Engraved oak doors were inset into the wall.

Gods below, that had been a close call. If my dark angel had come out, Ruadan would be trying to kill me right now.

I sucked in another long breath, and Ruadan turned to look at me. Droplets of water peaked his lashes.

He pulled a lever on the floor, and the sound of shifting stone filled the chamber. The bottom of the hatch closed.

I peered down at myself, at the blood dripping off my body.

"You're injured," said Ruadan.

"Was it all the blood that tipped you off?" I gasped. "You look a bit winded."

An arched eyebrow. "*I* look a bit winded?" Ruadan knelt by my side.

As soon as I looked down at my own arm, the pain from the wounds came roaring into my consciousness, and I gasped. It looked worse than I realized. "I'm so glad we can just portal out of this place."

Already, his healing magic was snaking over my skin, shimmering violet that began healing the ragged injury. He traced his fingertips over the wounds as he healed me, and his magic tingled up my arm.

"Are you nervous?" I asked. We'd come to save his mother. What sort of state would she be in after years of captivity, under Baleros's care?

"About what?"

"About seeing your mum after she's been imprisoned for fifteen years. Seems kind of like a big moment."

He shot me a surprised look, then focused on my arm again. "I hadn't thought about what we might find. I've been unwilling to expect that she might really be alive."

"You haven't thought about her because you don't want to be disappointed." I knew a thing or two about protecting your heart.

"She's the one who gave me over to Baleros when I was three. We never had a warm relationship, but I used to think she was a literal goddess." A line furrowed between his eyebrows, and he seemed lost in his own thoughts. "I made her wreaths out of apple blossoms and clover, threaded with silk ribbons. They were my offerings to her."

My lips twitched in a smile, warmth pooling in my chest. "Did she wear them?"

"No." His magic caressed my skin.

I *really* wanted to see Ruadan making a wreath out of flowers. "If you made me one, I'd wear it."

A smiled played over his lips for just a moment. "Do you actually want one?"

"Of course."

He met my gaze for a moment, his expression guarded, then focused on my arm again. At last, all the skin had healed.

As much as I'd thought about protecting my heart, I needed him close just for another moment. I wrapped my arms around his neck, pulling him in for a tight hug. I indulged for a second in his smell, in the feel of his skin against me. For an instant, his hand found the small of my back.

Then, he pulled away from me.

I crossed my arms, still catching my breath. "Do you think we'll find any more wyverns on the other side?" I asked.

I pressed my ear to the oak door, listening. It took only a moment before I realized the sheer pointlessness of trying to hear through a stone, airtight chamber wall.

Ruadan sniffed the air. "I have no idea. If it's anything we can't kill, I'll create a portal to get out of here."

He pushed on the oak door, and it groaned open, sliding against the rough floor. Ruadan's silver sphere shot into the room, but the darkness swallowed it up.

I took a tentative step inside after him. The air smelled of damp sediment, a hint of sulfur, and brine. A harsh sound rasped in the air around us, and a dank breeze lifted my hair.

How, exactly, was there a breeze in an airtight chamber?

The air whispered around me, and I was certain I heard the word *repent* in it, but I could see fuck-all. I gripped my sword tighter, totally unsure what to do in this situation. I was starting to feel nostalgic for my gladiator days. Granted, I had lived in a cage, but at least I'd got to fight monsters I could see in the open air.

From behind, a slimy limb snaked over my chest, and I whirled, swinging my sword. It sliced through the air, hitting nothing.

So, this is how it would be. We'd be fighting intangible wraiths in the dark.

Long, bony fingers tore at my hair. I pivoted again, but my sword slashed only air.

Then, from behind, a slithering hand covered my mouth, my nose, pinning me in place. Wet lips at my ear whispered, "Liora."

My heart skipped a beat. I couldn't let Ruadan hear my real name. I jabbed wildly behind me with my elbow, but my blows helplessly hit the air.

"Liora," the creature whispered again. What the fuck was this thing made of? Just disembodied arms and a wet mouth? "Liora," she whispered, a cold tongue licking at my ear. "You're far from home. You've lost your way, haven't you?"

Rage simmered under the surface, a roiling volcano ready to erupt.

The creature jammed her clammy fingers into my mouth, gagging me. They tasted of salty sediment and moss. Choking, I bit down hard on them, but she didn't seem to care, and she thrust her arm further into my throat. I couldn't breathe, and her moist flesh was invading me, stealing my air. A long, cold tongue licked up my neck, and I feared I'd vomit with her hand in my mouth. I wanted to rip her to pieces, but I couldn't grasp anything. She shoved her hand in farther, and I could feel the bile rising in my throat, threatening to explode.

"You know the truth, don't you, Liora?" Her voice was rising, my name loud on her tongue. What the hells was Ruadan doing right now? "You know what really happened that day, don't you?"

An image burst in my mind of red hair, blood streaming over pale skin—a trickle from red lips.

Rage erupted in a flash of white light, and in the next moment, I'd ripped her arms off of me. Now, my fist was hitting real flesh, fast as a storm wind. I pounded the creature, breaking bones, breaking skin. Then, I swung for her with my sword, the blade carving bone, carving flesh.

She kept whispering my name, over and over, until, at last … she went silent. Something heavy and wet fell to the floor.

Ruadan's silver sphere bloomed in the air again, casting its light over my attacker. I was surprised to see that she looked beautiful—a pale little waif with silver hair. The only thing animal about her was her long claws. She wore a long, green gown, and waxy limbs lay across the stone floor. I'd battered the shit out of her. Had that delicate little thing nearly killed me?

I glanced up at Ruadan. Two waifs lay at his feet, their eyes gaping. His kills had been cleaner—two simple snapped necks, jaws hanging open.

I caught my breath. "Did you hear any of that?" I asked.

"Any of what?" His voice sounded sharp. Something had definitely rattled him.

The bit about my name being Liora. "What she said to me. Did you hear it?"

He shook his head, his skin paler than normal. Whatever they'd said to him had unnerved him.

Clack, clack, clack.... A new sound echoed from the shadows. It sounded like bones tapping against each other. I tightened my grip on the sword, my palm slicked with blood from the waif.

A chill danced up the back of my neck as I stepped farther into the hall.

Ruadan whispered a spell, calling up another orb of silver light—larger this time. It floated further into the hall, until it cast its eerie light over a tall figure.

A throned woman sat before us—a silver cloak, a crown of black horns, dark feathers that swooped up from her collar. She held a silver scepter, its top crowned with an opalescent dome. Her eyes had the same opalescent sheen.

From one hand, her long, black nails clacked against the throne's stone arms. Her skin looked like marble, and ravens fluttered around her head.

I swallowed hard. Was this Ruadan's mum? No wonder he used to think she was a goddess. *I* believed she was a goddess, and I'd only just seen her for the first time. I could not imagine this woman being thrilled by a gift of floral wreaths from a little boy, and the thought of tiny Ruadan trying to impress her made me want to wrap my arms around him again.

"Mother," said Ruadan.

CHAPTER 18

*S*he arched a thin, white eyebrow. "Ruadan. Fifteen years." Her voice sounded angry and calm at the same time, strangely dissonant. "It took you fifteen years to find me."

"I didn't know you were alive. Baleros staged your death."

Clack ... clack.... Her nails beat out a steady rhythm. She sniffed. "It's almost as if you learned nothing from him." The ravens fluttered about her head.

How old was this woman? She wasn't an ordinary fae, but seemed old as time itself. I felt like she'd been on earth long enough that she'd started to meld with it. She seemed a force of nature more than an individual. This was not a woman with ordinary feelings and desires.

Her head swiveled, a birdlike movement. When her pale eyes landed on me, I had to force myself to hold my ground instead of scuttling back. She sniffed the air again, her expression darkening. "What did you bring with you, Ruadan?"

Force of nature or not, I wasn't sure I liked the woman's tone.

I cocked a hip. "It's *who.* Not what. In the English language, when you're talking about a person, you say *who.*"

A heavy silence fell over the hall.

"My name is Arianna," I said.

"Knight of the Shadow Fae," added Ruadan.

Queen Macha cocked her head, studying me like a bird of prey studies a mouse. "But that's not her real name, is it?"

My heart sputtered. *Oh, bloody hells.* Not only had I stumbled into the weirdest godsdamned family reunion since Edward IV drowned his brother in a bucket of Malmsey wine, but this queen was about to unveil my secrets.

Ruadan cut me a sharp look. "Not your real name," he repeated, a hint of steel in his tone.

Now, I had two ancient, terrifying fae staring at me and waiting for an explanation. I swallowed hard, my mouth dry. How much did she know? And *how* did she know anything about me?

"What makes you say that?" I asked in a voice so soft I could hardly hear it myself.

Clack, clack, clack.... "It's quite simple. I always know when someone is lying. You, little thing, are lying to my son."

My stomach dropped. Still, she didn't know much.

I stole a quick glance back at Ruadan, whose violet eyes pierced me to the core. Was that betrayal I read in them?

"Why are we talking about me? Shouldn't you two hug or something? I mean, it's been a while." I made my voice sound jovial. "Yay! You've got the gang back together."

Two sets of immortal eyes trained on me, the only sound the flapping of the ravens' wings.

I cleared my throat. "Or not. Whatever. I mean, I have a weird relationship with my—" *parents.* I let the word die on my tongue. No reason to dredge that up right now. "You know what? Never mind. I like your ravens, Queen Macha. I'm thinking of getting some of my own."

The birds swooped before her face as she stared at me, still as her throne.

"We should probably leave here," I offered. "Before something comes to kill us. I think that's the most important thing right now. And then we have some very important questions to ask about Baleros."

Queen Macha rose from her throne. The woman was only about five feet tall, but somehow, she managed to loom over us. "Yes. Son, open a portal before the wyverns return."

As if on cue, a wyvern's screech rumbled off the stone.

Ruadan touched his throat, and his World Key began glowing with pale gold. Already, the floor began trembling, until fissures opened in the dark stone. The flagstones crumbled and fractured. Dark, star-flecked waters burst from the floor, rushing in a whirlpool.

I leapt in with the others, plunging into frigid water once more.

* * *

IN THE INSTITUTE'S throne room, I hugged myself tightly, trying to warm up. Aengus tossed me a towel.

"Is no one going to ask the queen how she's doing?" I asked.

All eyes in the hall turned to me—Aengus, Ruadan, and the queen.

Clack, clack.... The queen sat in Ruadan's stone throne, and she tapped her claws on the arm.

"Queen Macha," I began, "given that you were imprisoned by a maniac for the past fifteen years, how are you feeling?"

She blinked. "Hungry."

I turned to Aengus. "See? It helps to ask these questions. Maybe we can get some sort of food."

"It's not that sort of hunger," said Ruadan.

Did I want to know? "What do you mean?"

Queen Macha lifted her chin. "I feast on the spirits of my defeated enemies, those fallen in battle. I feast on victory in war. The blood of the fallen nourishes me like a mother's milk. It's been a long time since I've ripped an enemy's filthy head from his body and drank from his demise. I long to choke Baleros with his own entrails. I would like to ram his skull up his own arse, and feed from his humiliating subjugation."

My jaw dropped for a moment. So *this* was Ruadan's mum.

I scrubbed a hand over my mouth. "We will work on that. Maybe after a regular snack of cheese and crackers or something to take the edge off?"

Ruadan was pacing the room, arms folded. His shadows claimed the air around him, and the room felt as cold as it had in the tunnels. It seemed as if a reunion with his long-lost mother hadn't done much to calm his nerves. "Queen Macha, we need information about where to find Baleros. We have nothing to go on, and we're running out of time."

She sighed. "He kept me alone in a room by myself for fifteen years. Underwater. He came to see me only twice."

"And what can you tell us?" Ruadan prodded.

"He came once to tell me that he was going to kill you, and another time to try to mate with me. I divested him of his entrails, and he did not make that mistake a second time. Unfortunately, Emerazel, flaming gutter-bitch of the fire hell, revived him after I slaughtered him."

Ruadan's magic whipped the air around him. "I know you learned something from his visits."

"Yes. He smelled of yews."

Ruadan's head snapped up, as if this was meaningful. "Yews."

"The tree?" I asked. What in the world…?

It was at this point that I noticed Melusine had crossed into the room. She stumbled into the center of the hall, her blue hair tangled over her shoulders. She held up a hand, like she was in class waiting to be called on. "I know this one," she blurted. "Yews. The sacred tree of Arubian."

"Arubian," I repeated, adding nothing helpful whatsoever to the discussion.

Melusine raised her hand again. "Yeah, I can actually field this one, too. I've been doing my research on the fomoire. I hear the name Arubian, I know he's fomoire. Death fae. Fomoire feed off unpleasant things, right?"

A spark of understanding lit in my mind. "Unpleasant things like the spirits of the defeated?" I turned to the queen. "*You're* fomoire as well?"

A dark smile curled Queen Macha's lips. "You didn't realize that my son was fomoire?" Harsh laughter burst from her throat. "Silly cow."

My pulse sped up.

Darkness rushed from Ruadan's body, slamming across the room. Silence fell again as the shadows dissipated. "Baleros." His voice as cold as ice. "We need to know about Baleros. You think he's working with Arubian?"

We were here to talk about Baleros, but the question lingered in my mind—what did Ruadan feed from? Seemed like we were both keeping secrets.

Queen Macha tapped the throne with her long finger-nails. "Arubian has a fortress in East London. It's glamoured. An old cemetery, an abandoned church. A bunch of filthy human hoboes sit outside the glamour. If you can find your way through the glamour, you can find the palace. Baleros has a tendency to feed fomoire with human sacrifices. The fomoire become dependent on him for supplies, then loyal to him. I suspect Arubian is one of his generals, yes."

"What else do we need to know about him?" I asked.

"Arubian hunts the night skies, feasting off dread," said Ruadan.

I shrugged. "I mean, he sounds fun, I guess. Sounds like your kind of people. Since you're all fomoire."

Ruadan cut me a sharp look.

Melusine raised her hand again. "I got this one, too. One, he's got a whole pack of dogs, takes 'em right through the night sky. Two, he hates fire. He sees flames, he gets scared. Three, you're gonna need a strong fire demon to get through his glamour. Burn a hole right in it with the flames of Emerazel. Problem is, you're all Shadow Fae. Fire's not really your thing. Am I right?"

Ciara. We needed Ciara for this. I raked a hand through my hair. "Okay. We have to access some fire magic."

It was nearly dawn, and I desperately wanted to go to sleep, but there wasn't enough time to take a break.

"We don't have time to find a fire demon," said Ruadan.

Queen Macha cocked her head. "What exactly is the rush? What aren't you telling me?"

"I'll get you up to speed," I said. "Baleros nailed a hand to the door with a note, and it said we have a day to deliver Ruadan to him, or he'll unleash a plague. To prove he's serious, he already unleashed a small one. He also killed Grand Master Savus and stole the mist army. Your son is the new Grand Master, minus an army. Baleros has acquired a whole bunch of human soldiers who think they're dead, and they have a terrible habit of blowing themselves up."

"He's been a very naughty boy," said the queen. "How did he unleash the Plague, exactly? I know of no creature who can do that except the Angel of Death. And Adonis is locked in another realm. Or did he escape?"

Ruadan stepped forward. "It's possible Adonis was able to get out of his locked world, or that he slipped through the portal after my attack. Both are my enemies, both on my kill list. They may have formed an alliance."

Darkness swarmed in my mind, and the scent of myrrh pooled around me. My father's scent.

Maybe I'd be seeing him soon.

CHAPTER 19

o. It couldn't be happening—they couldn't be working together.

"We have no idea how Baleros plans to do it," I said a little too sharply. "Just that he does. It could be a magical spell for all we know. He used magic to create the jackdaws."

"The strategy is simple," said Queen Macha. "Baleros is a traitor to the Shadow Fae and an enemy of Emain. We must amass an army of all the world's Shadow Fae and surround Arubian's palace." Her cheeks reddened, eyes gleaming. "We crush our enemies. Drag Baleros out, bring him to me so I may tear out his spine and whip his arse with it. I will need to feast on his ignominious defeat!"

Her shouts rang off the stone walls. I wasn't entirely sure she was thinking clearly right now.

Ruadan shook his head. "That's not a good idea. Baleros has a lumen stone. If he sees us coming with an entire army behind us, he'll be gone within a heartbeat. We have to go in silently, move in the shadows."

"We don't even know that he's there for certain," said

Aengus. "If we keep hidden, we might be able to find out more information."

Queen Macha's lips curled back from her teeth. "I. Am. Hungry." This time, her voice came out like a low hiss. I had the distinct impression that she couldn't think clearly when she was hungry.

"Fire magic," I said again. "I know where we can get a demon."

Aengus glared at me. "How will we summon this demon?"

"Mobile phone. Get the portal ready, Ruadan. This is happening."

* * *

AENGUS, Ruadan, and I stood under an oak tree, bodies dripping wet. I shuddered, hugging myself. I *really* wanted some fae technomancer to create a type of portal that did not involve icy water, so we could arrive somewhere dry for once. But that was a problem for another day—a day when we were not facing an apocalyptic event within the next sixteen hours.

A pale flash of movement caught my attention through the trees, a glimpse of ginger hair.

I smiled as Ciara crossed to us, her feet crunching over the leaves. I wrapped my arms around her, then she cast a wary look at the two other Shadow Fae.

"It's okay, Ciara," I said. "We're all allies here. No one is arresting anyone, anyway."

"Well, in that case, it's good to see you all. How's the palace? I've been living under a car. I'm not complaining, but I have been living literally underneath a car. Not even in it. I can't get the doors open, so I just crawl between the tires. This morning I had to fight a pigeon for a chicken bone. So that was my day. But I bet the palace is real nice. Real beds. Right? You all sleep in real beds? Do you have to fight diseased scavenger birds for your food, or can you just eat it right off the plate?"

"Is there a point to this?" asked Aengus. "I thought you said she was a fire demon."

"We'll get you some food when we're done with this," I promised. "Unlike Ruadan, Ciara feeds on actual food."

I didn't know why that had come out so angrily. What was I doing getting mad at Ruadan for keeping secrets? I had plenty of my own.

Ruadan kept his eyes on Ciara, ignoring me completely. "The Shadow Fae are promising you immunity from your transgressions if you will aid us in our mission."

She nodded. "Yeah, sure. But I hope you're serious about the food."

"And a bed," I offered.

"In a locked room," Ruadan added. "We can't have fire demons roaming around the Institute."

"Locked room is better than living under a car," she muttered. "What's the job?"

"We need to get through the glamour outside the palace," said Ruadan. "And we need your fire magic for that."

She scratched a freckled cheek. "I don't really have great control over it, per se."

"Look," said Aengus. "We know literally no other fire demons, or we would have asked them. You'll just have to do your best."

"To be honest, the only time I used it was when Baleros had captured me."

I thought I understood where she was going with this. "You thought you were about to die then, right?" Exactly how my death powers worked.

Her brow furrowed. "I did, yeah. Obviously we can't make that—"

"Ruadan can make it happen," I interrupted.

"If I know that he's faking it, I won't really believe I'm about to die."

"Trust me," I said. "He will dredge up your worst fears and just shove them down your throat until your mind is about to break. It's one of his favorite pastimes."

Did he feed off fear, like Arubian?

"When we get through the glamour," said Ruadan, "we will find ourselves in the grounds that surround Arubian's palace. I don't know what to expect, except that Baleros supplies him with humans to feed off. We may find Baleros within these grounds, or we can interrogate Arubian until he tells us more."

Aengus's green eyes pierced the dark. "Once we get through the glamour, we'll need to be discreet and blend in with whatever is going on around us."

"And while you're blending in," added Ruadan, "I'll dash around the palace, searching for Baleros."

Ciara cross her arms, beaming. "If there is one thing I'm good at, it's being a normal human. I believed I was a normal human for years, didn't know any different till I blew up in the Tower. I spent years doing normal human things like drawing my friends on the wall and hosting pimento cheese parties."

The two Shadow Fae nodded, and I didn't alert them to the fact that even when Ciara had believed she was human, literally no one had thought she was normal. They had no idea.

"See?" I said. "She'll be fine. Totally normal human."

"Let's go." Ruadan took off into the forest. Since we were supposed to be discreet, we had no orb of silver light to lead our way here. In any case, dawn would be breaking soon.

"Why do you always carry that bag with you?" asked Aengus.

"Because, Aengus. For eight years, I had nothing, and now I carry my own sweets with me."

"Sweets," he snorted.

I pulled one of the straps off my shoulder and shoved my hand into the bag. I snatched a cherry lollipop and handed it to him. As we walked in the forest, he unwrapped it and frowned at it. It became clear to me that Aengus had never had a lollipop before.

"You lick it, Aengus."

He waggled an eyebrow at me like I'd said something completely obscene, which I suppose was understandable. Then, he stuck out his tongue and licked the lollipop. Quite frankly, it *did* look completely obscene the way he did it, and I suppressed a smile.

Ciara held out a hand, and I gave her a butterscotch lollipop.

Around us, thick tree roots covered the path, and dark shapes lined either side of our way. As the first ruddy rays of dawn began to brighten the sky, I started to make out the shapes more clearly. We were walking past old, Victorian graves—crooked statues, broken crosses lining our path. At one point, this must have been a stately cemetery, well-tended. But over the years, the trees and shrubs had started to break the stones apart, shift the bodies out of place. Time had run riot around here, the ground bulging and disturbing the dead.

The plants here looked unfamiliar—their stems thick and tough, spiked. I had the sense that they grew only over places of death—fomoire in their own way, feasting off misery.

We skirted the edge of a clearing, where a man sat smoking a pipe. The pink glow of dawn illuminated his scruffy face, and he was singing a Beyoncé song to himself. He didn't notice us at all.

Just on the other side of the clearing stood an abandoned church. When had it last been used? World War II, maybe? The windows had been smashed and boarded up, probably bombed in the war.

I was about to move on when Ruadan stopped, tracing his fingertips over the air. "We're here. The glamour."

My mother had been an expert in glamour, but that magical gene had passed me by. I couldn't even see it.

Ruadan turned, surveying the brightening forest around us.

"Anyone around?" I asked.

He narrowed his eyes. "Just the drunk human we passed. We're fine." He turned his attention to Ciara. "We'll need your fire to get through this."

She popped her lollipop out of her mouth. "You gonna hit me with your scare magic?"

Aengus and I took a few paces back—then a few more, to avoid the intensity of Ruadan's magic. I wanted to get hit with neither fire nor terror right now.

When I was about twenty feet away from them, darkness bloomed around Ruadan, the shadows tinged with faint glimmers of stars.

Ciara started to shake, her jaw dropping. She clamped a trembling hand over her mouth and screamed into it. Then, flames erupted from her body. Ruadan shifted away.

A burst of fire climbed twelve feet in the air, a wall of flames. The air hissed and sizzled. Through the inferno, a gap opened up in the glamour, large enough to drive a train through.

"Now!" said Ruadan. "Get through!"

Ciara was still screaming into her hand.

I ran toward the gap and pushed her in, wincing as her

body seared my palms a little. We rushed through the opening into a vast, grassy field. A carpet of wood-sorrel and yellow archangels grew among the tall grasses.

And at the far end of the field loomed a palace of white stone.

CHAPTER 20

*T*let out a long, slow breath. I'd never had any idea that this was here.

"Nice work, Ciara," I said. Then, I leaned in and whispered, "What did Ruadan make you see?"

She licked her lips. "Fox in a wedding dress, walking on her hind legs through the forest. Her true love left her at the altar, and she wanted revenge. She carried a bouquet of dried lilies."

I frowned, unsettled. "That's very ... specific."

"She wanted to carve my eyes straight out of my head with a whittling knife," she trilled, trying to sound cheerful. "Like my grandaddy did to that fox I caught in a trap. He wanted to teach me a lesson. Golly, have you ever heard a fox scream?"

"Let's not talk about this anymore." Inside Ciara's head was a very dark place, and I didn't want to spend much time in there.

Up ahead, a small crowd of people were stumbling over the grass under the rose and violet sky. I could hear their laughter from here.

Were they having *fun*? Considering Arubian fed off terror, I had expected to find horror here, not laughter.

They moved around each other, laughter growing louder. The only thing strange about them was an oddly lumbering gait, as if they had weights attached to their feet.

As we moved closer, I started to make out their clothing —tiny shorts, sparkly tops, flashes of rainbow, striped socks pulled up to their knees. It took me a little while to piece together what was going on here.

What in the world…?

Arms whirling, they moved over the grass, giggling.

Ruadan leaned down, whispering close to my ear. "Can you help me interpret this? I don't understand."

"Rollerskating," I whispered. "I think we may be going to a roller disco."

I bit my lip, imagining Ruadan in a pair of tiny striped shorts and rollerskates. I tried so hard to suppress the laughter that I snorted.

He shot me a sharp look. "What's wrong with you?"

I shook my head. "I'm just really looking forward to this blending in part. But we're going to need to steal their clothes, so can you put them to sleep?"

No sooner were the words out of my mouth than violet-tinged magic spiraled out of Ruadan's chest. It snaked over the grass and swept around the humans. Instantly, his sleep magic began to take effect. Their arms windmilled around for a few moments until they toppled over into the grass.

When we reached them, I surveyed their prone bodies and their tight roller disco clothes. I looked up at Ruadan and Aengus. "I don't think any of this will fit you two."

"These clothes are ridiculous," muttered Ruadan.

I started stripping the shorts off one of the girls. I did my best to shield my body and hers as I traded my drenched black dress for her sparkly halter top and shorts. Then, I slid out of my shoes and pulled on her rollerskates. I was vaguely aware of Ruadan rifling through my bug-out bag, but I kept my attention focused on trying to keep my nipples hidden while I slipped into the halter top.

When I looked up again, Ciara had dressed herself in a red bikini top and glittery blue shorts, along with a pair of rollerskates. Already, she looked like a proper expert, shaking her hips to a distant beat as she rolled over the grass.

Ruadan and Aengus had simply ripped the wheel sets off two pairs of skates, and secured them to their shoes with the duct tape from my bag.

I frowned at them. They were still dressed like fae. We needed a hipster rollerskating look here.

I pulled an elastic band off my wrist, then crossed to Ruadan. "Lean down."

"What?"

"Just do it, Ruadan. Trust me."

He leaned down a bit, as if bowing, and I gathered his soft blond hair up into a messy man bun. I took a step back to survey it. That was all it took to make him look like a hipster.

"Good," I said. "Perfect."

He growled low. He wasn't sure what I'd done to him or why, but he didn't like it.

I opened up my bug-out bag for a quick review of my weapons before we went into battle. A few daggers, aerosolized deodorant, and a lighter.

When I looked up again, I found Ciara hacking away at Aengus's trousers to create a pair of short shorts. He glowered at her as she worked.

I took a deep breath, my pulse already racing in anticipation of our encounter with Arubian. I had to come to this thing sword-free. That was the problem about covert missions—you could never bring your favorite weapons, and you had to rely on a backpack full of knives and deodorant.

"Let's go," said Ruadan.

I rolled over the grass, using my arms to steady myself a bit. It took me a few minutes before I was moving smoothly, and then I started to get into it. I could have used these things in the gladiator ring.

Charcoal-grey clouds began gathering on the horizon, blotting out the rising sun. They seemed to be moving unnaturally fast, roiling and writhing like a living thing.

I glanced over at Ruadan, who was already ripping the wheels off the bottom of his shoes. I should've known that wouldn't last long.

"What about your disguise?" I asked.

"I'm the Wraith," he said. "I don't need a disguise. No one can see me, and I'll be mostly sneaking around the palace unseen."

Fair enough.

Aengus looked furious, stumbling over the grass in his rollerskates and tiny shorts. Ciara had also forced his enormous chest into a rainbow halter top.

A flash of white lightning cracked the darkening sky, followed by a boom of thunder. The air felt charged, heavy.

As we moved closer to the palace, another flash speared the sky—horizontal this time, slashing the dark clouds open with its light.

"Heat lightning," said Ciara.

I frowned. "It's not even that hot."

I rolled over the bumpy terrain, and pale flashes of light streaked faster across the sky. The hair on my nape stood on end.

By the time we reached the palace itself, the lightning had picked up pace, pulsing in the clouds as fast as a heartbeat, fast as neuronal connections. The palace itself looked completely undefended—no moat, no gate, just a gaping open archway that led into a courtyard. Through the archway, I could hear the deep, throbbing bass of a disco song. The sound of the Bee Gees seemed an odd contrast to the grotesque, humanoid gargoyles looming over the archway. They jutted from the ancient palace walls. Men with gaping leers, grinning as they pulled open their mouths or ripped out their own hearts.

"Ummm…" said Ciara. "I'm not really sure what's going on here."

"Neither am I," I said. "That's why we're in disguise. We blend in, make ourselves look like weak humans until we can figure out … what the hells is happening."

Warm candlelight flickered in some of the palace windows. Was Baleros in one of those rooms? I was tempted to rush into the palace and tear the place apart until we found him, but like Ruadan had said, he could never see us coming. We had to know exactly where he was before we attacked.

Just before we crossed under the arch, the sound of baying hounds turned my head. I held my breath. Above us, a glowing figure streaked beneath the clouds, lightning flashing around him. He wore a dark cloak, and his eyes burned orange, like Mars—so bright I could see them even from here. Enormous, white phantom hounds pounded the sky, pulling his chariot and leaving streaks of pearly white in their wake.

I exhaled slowly. This fomoire was definitely not an ordinary fae.

"Is that Arubian?" I whispered.

"That's him," said Ruadan.

His path began to arc above the palace, a wide, graceful swoop.

"You three blend in," said Ruadan. "I'm going to search the palace. Don't do anything until I come back." Ruadan's enormous form grew indistinct, dark mist whirling around him.

My muscles tensed completely as we moved toward the courtyard. Arubian had covered the entire courtyard with a hardwood floor, and lights flashed over the rink. Partygoers skated around, laughing with each other. The Bee Gees song "Massachusetts" blared over a speaker, echoing off the palace's stone walls. On the outskirts of the parquet floor, lanterns jutted from the earth, at least six feet high, flashing with pink, green, blue….

I glanced at the palace walls, which formed a square around the rink. Was Baleros in one of those wings?

A blond woman with pigtails glided over the floor, ducking down low and sticking out a leg in a move I thought might be called "shoot the duck."

We rolled onto the disco floor—all of us except Ruadan, who I could no longer see.

The partygoers were singing along to the Bee Gees, something about the lights going out in Massachusetts. I thought Arubian fed off dread? Where was the dread? These people were having fun.

Aengus rolled headfirst into the crowd, having absolutely no control over the skates. He plowed into a group of laughing women, who helped him up, shrieking with delight. One of them grabbed him by the arms and swung him around in a circle, arm over arm. She was laughing uproariously, while he had a look of terror on his face. The Bee Gees warbled on.

Ciara grabbed my arm, and we took off over the floor. I had the sense that she'd spent her American youth on a pair of skates, because she was soon slipping away from me to roll backward like an expert, singing along to the disco, arms outstretched.

Bits of hail began raining down, catching in the colored lights of the rink like disco sequins falling from the sky. It was summer. Why was it hailing? I didn't care, because it was beautiful. I had a strange, giddy feeling, and I wanted to stay here all night, laughing with my new friends.

I tried a turn, skating backwards to the sounds of falsetto singing.

But when Arubian cut over the cloudy sky again—a ghostly flash of white—my nerves juddered. What exactly did he do with these people?

But the music seemed to mesmerize me, and I quickly forgot about him again. I tried a twirl on my skates, gripping onto the straps of my backpack.

Another flash of white—swooping closer this time—and my throat tightened. The melodious singing of the Bee Gees floated over the crowd, and Arubian's hounds began to descend. None of the humans seemed to notice the mood shifting, the air thinning. They didn't seem to notice the music changing and growing more dissonant.

It was only at that point that I noticed the streaks of red on the parquet floor—smears of blood among the melting hail. A severed finger. My stomach flipped.

Still, around me, the skaters danced on, smiling. I rolled closer to Ciara, then grabbed her arm.

"Ciara," I whispered. "Get ready for some disturbing shit."

"What do we do?" she asked.

"Nothing until Ruadan gets back. We stay alive, and that's about it."

A man with a potbelly and a yellow T-shirt skated past us. He twirled before us, smiling at his own prowess, then he looked me up and down. He grabbed his crotch, expertly skating backward. "Can I show you a little skating move I like to call the slap and tickle?"

I blocked him out completely, eyes flicking to the skies again as I caught a glimpse of Arubian charging for him. The Bee Gees sounded darker now, and my pulse began to race faster. The hounds were heading for the creepy man who'd just been leering at us, and he didn't seem to notice.

I grabbed Ciara's arm, and we skated away from him, blending into the crowd. I stole a quick look back at the man.

My jaw dropped as one of the hounds tore into his leg, and his heavy body slammed onto the parquet floor.

Now, a few people in the crowd began shrieking, finally noticing that something was amiss.

I gritted my teeth, willing myself not to jump into the fray. I was here to gain information about Baleros, and I wouldn't get anything if I tried to save every random, dick-head human.

The hounds backed away from the man, but they growled at him as he tried to stand.

Arubian swooped lower, and I caught a glimpse of his face—his skin the color of bone, features a beautiful mask of death.

CHAPTER 21

The crowd's screams trembled over my skin, and I mingled among the humans, watching from a distance as Arubian touched down on the parquet floor. A dark grin twisted his features, and he reached out a long, bony hand toward the man. The man's screams ripped through the air, and he scrambled up to his skates. With his damaged leg, he was off balance, now, and he kept stumbling as he tried to roll away. He left a shiny trail of blood behind him.

Arubian flicked his wrist, and one of the hounds snarled, lunging for the human again. The dog ripped at the man's arm, tearing into his flesh. The human went down hard.

Then, the hound transformed into a lean but muscled two-legged form—with pointed dog ears and sharp canines. As long claws grew from his fingertips, the shifter stalked his prey. The man was crawling backward like a crab.

Arubian glowed with silver light, his face a picture of ecstasy. Here was a fomoire, feeding in his natural habitat. It was repulsive, frankly.

The hound shifter lunged, striking his claws across the

man's belly, opening him up. Bile rose in my throat, and I turned away from the sound of the screaming.

I'd seen my fair share of carnage in my days—hells, I'd delivered my fair share of carnage. But this seemed particularly cruel and drawn out. I'd hacked through necks, stopped hearts. I'd poisoned people with my mind. So why did I feel a sense of superiority? I guess my kills were fast, and I never relished my enemies' torment, never drew out their pain or their horror just for the fun of it. I was practical—Arubian was a sadist.

Was Ruadan? What the hells did he get up to in his free time? Did he have an underground nightclub somewhere, complete with a disco ball, where he tortured people to death on Saturday nights?

Despite the horror on the parquet floor, no one was leaving the roller disco. Another fae trick—trapping the victims in the rink just by screwing with their minds.

The white hounds circled the roller parquet floor, teeth bared. Were the Bee Gees still playing? Gods help us all, this was disturbing.

I rolled on, pretending like I had no idea what was happening.

I cast a quick glance back to Arubian, who now stood hunched over the dying man, lovingly stroking a bony fingertip over the human's lips like a mother hushing a baby. There was hardly anything left of the poor guy, and yet no one was delivering a mercy stroke. Blood pooled below him on the shiny floor.

I couldn't say I was learning much here. Had Ruadan found anything? Because we were running out of time, and I wasn't getting us any closer to Baleros.

As if hearing my thoughts, a dark form flickered by my side, and Ruadan's piney scent curled around me.

His breath warmed my ear. "Baleros isn't here. We need

to interrogate the fomoire. Take out the dogs first. Then we go for Arubian."

I nodded, slipping my backpack off my shoulders. Good. I got to kill again.

Arubian was lost in his dark ecstasy, his body glowing. He didn't notice when I reached into my backpack, grabbing onto a sheathed knife. He didn't notice when I pulled out my tool belt and wrapped it around my waist, or when I shoved the dagger in it. I pulled out a lighter and a can of deodorant, slipping them into my belt, too.

I scanned the crowd, watching as they tried to scatter. Half the skaters were crying, terrified, and the other half were still laughing and oblivious.

The rest of the hounds began transforming, bodies elongating until they were shaped like men—only with snouts and long ears.

After what I'd just seen, I was hungry for their blood, and a smile already curled my own lips. *You like hunting the weak, don't you? You like to torment those who can't fight back. Let's see how you like messing with me.*

I didn't have to choose which shifter to go for, because one of them already had his sights set on me. Smiling, I skated away from him, luring him closer and swaying my hips. I moved fluidly over the floor, weaving between the crowd. This was a strange sort of seduction, one that would end in his death.

He prowled closer, then shifted back into his hound form to run, lighting-fast. As he leapt for me, I pulled out the lighter and can of deodorant. I flicked the lighter, sprayed the can, and flames burst into the air.

He yelped, jumping back, and burst back into his humanoid form. On the floor, he snarled, holding his face. I circled him on my skates, reaching for my dagger.

I hadn't quite pulled it out when his claws raked through my chest. Pain pierced me.

Fucker was *fast,* and he had much longer arms. I'd have to keep blasting him with fire. Gritting my teeth, I unleashed another burst of flame, igniting his white hair. While he was busy covering his skull, I lunged in with my iron dagger. I plunged it between two of his ribs, then pulled it out again to thrust it up his rib cage, tilting it toward his heart.

He slumped to the ground, dead.

And *that's* how you kill someone, civilized-like. No need to draw it out.

Already, another shifter was charging for me in his hound form. I gripped the blood soaked knife and tossed it at the oncoming hound.

Unfortunately, he managed to shift just a bit at the last moment, and the dagger caught him in the shoulder instead of in his chest. I hadn't even slowed him down.

Shit.

I needed a *sword,* godsdamn it. I gripped the deodorant and blasted him with fire, but he wasn't dumb enough to come close when I had my makeshift flamethrower. It wouldn't kill him.

Baleros's fifteenth law of power: Always use your surroundings.

My gaze darted to the colorful lanterns that lined the rink, and I sped over to one of them. I gripped it with both hands, ripping it from the ground.

I grinned at the sight of its pointed tip, but my joy was short-lived. Powerful, white arms gripped me from behind, knocking me off balance, claws digging into the bare skin at my sides. I slammed onto my back, just barely managing to hang onto my makeshift weapon.

Two on one—they didn't care for fair fights.

How many people had they tortured to death? How many

women—just like me, only weaker? The hound shifters liked to dominate.

From the ground, I gripped the metal lantern stake and swung for the legs of the closest shifter. I took him down, then leapt up to my skates—nearly falling off balance, as I'd forgotten about the wheels. I whirled, slamming the stake into the next shifter's head. He faltered, but the shifters were strong, and I didn't take him down. Clutching my new weapon, I began skating away until I could even out my odds a little bit. Just out of range, I turned and hurled the stake like a spear. It slammed into one of the shifters, and he fell back hard to the ground.

My gaze flicked to Aengus, who was fighting with his dagger. He'd ripped the wheels off his shoes, and he pivoted to drive his blade into one of the shifters.

I didn't even know where the hells Ruadan was, but the trail of shifter corpses told me he was racking up a body count somewhere around here.

I snatched another lantern from the earth, and when one of the shifters came for me, I snarled and drove the tip into his heart before he could even reach me.

The hounds were closing in—some shaped like men, some like animals. Their snarls echoed all around me, and I turned in a circle to find that I'd been surrounded.

I am the twilight shadow that creeps over long grasses....

My death instinct began whispering through me, shoulder blades tingling.

I am the hunter who creeps up behind you.

One of the shifters lunged from behind, knocking me to the ground, face-down. Climbing all over me like I was the damn spoils of war, his teeth pierced the flesh at my throat. Pain screamed through my body. He was pawing at me, scoring my skin with his claws, and rage began to rise.

I'm not your prize. I will steal your food and your breath.

From the ground, I brought up my elbow hard into his ribs, cracking them so hard I must have broken them. Another slam from my elbow and he started to slide off me. When I stood again, I was gripping hard to the lantern. The shifters started to move in on me, eyes glowing.

I'm your last rasping breath.

I swung the lantern, carving its pointed tip through lungs, hearts, bellies—my body moving so fast my mind could hardly keep up. It wasn't me anymore; it was the dark angel. The euphoria of battle ignited me, and I felt my shoulder blades tingle.

I'm the darkness swaying beneath your feet.

CHAPTER 22

The pointed tip of the lantern found its way into a shifter's white neck, dark metal piercing ivory. With a roar, I ripped it free again, ready to take on the next shifter, my body buzzing. But when I scanned my surroundings, I found that the shifters were all dead.

I took in the rink. Arubian stood in the center of the floor, watching me. Ciara was hiding somewhere, I thought. Aengus was fighting off two hounds. By the archway, a shadow appeared to rip a shifter's heart out of his chest. That would be Ruadan.

I looked down at myself, and some of the death instinct slipped away from my body. Dark blood soaked my glittery disco clothes and my skates.

I was calming myself, now, but I felt rattled by the sense that my death instinct was growing stronger, desperate to break free. Maybe that's what happened when you spent too much energy trying to suppress something. Whatever you were trying to keep down would just ram you hard in the ribs until it got control again.

Shit.

Now, the humans were skating around the wounded bodies, some slipping on the blood. Most of them were crying, heaving for breath. And yet, it still seemed that they couldn't bring themselves to leave.

Arubian's eyes were locked on me and me alone.

I waited until I caught a glimpse of Ciara, red hair streaming behind her, before moving toward Arubian. As a fire demon, Ciara was supposed to be our real muscle here.

I gripped the lantern as I began to skate over to him, while Aengus and Ruadan moved behind him.

"You killed my hounds," he said quietly. Up close, I could smell the scent of yews.

Out of the shadows, Ruadan appeared, his violet eyes blazing. "Baleros. Where is he?"

Arubian pulled down his cowl to reveal dark hair slicked back on his head. His expression was much more amused than I'd expect from a man who'd just watched his henchmen massacred in his home.

"We're looking for Baleros," Aengus added. "Has he been feeding you these humans?"

"Where is he?" Ruadan asked, the air around him chilling.

"Ah. Baleros." Arubian was positively glowing with pearly light, beautiful as the moon itself.

Turning, he surveyed his domain. A few hunched servants had rushed out to mop up the gore with an efficiency that suggested they did this all the time. Arubian gestured at the remaining skaters, who were now clinging to each other, rolling past the carnage. "It's true, Baleros brings me these wonderful presents. These humans who keep me company, who stop me from starving."

Ciara stepped forward, holding up her hands to the sky. "I am a fire demon," she declared.

"Congratulations." Arubian didn't look particularly impressed, so the information about his fire fears might have been a bit misleading. He pulled a packet of cigarettes from his cloak and tapped them in his palm a few times. Then, he slid one from the pack, holding it out to Ciara. "Care to light this for me?"

She wrinkled her nose. "I don't really do that kind of thing."

This conversation had taken an unexpected turn, and I wasn't entirely clear how to get control again or how to instill the sort of terror we needed. Sighing, I pulled out a lighter from my tool belt, then lit his cigarette. Even the smoke smelled of yews.

As I tried to think of what to say, Ruadan disappeared into the shadows again.

Might as well get to the point. "Look, Arubian, can you tell us where to find him, or do we have to torture you with fire and lanterns? Those are your options."

"Not a giant fan of torture." Arubian shrugged. "And I *am* on a bit of a high from all the death." He blew a smoke ring into the air. "Fine, you didn't hear it from me, but I've heard a rumor that he's taken up residence in the old home built for Nan and Burly Hal. You know, before the awkward breakup."

"Who the fuck are Nan and Burly Hal?" I asked in my usual diplomatic tone.

Arubian's orange eyes burned into me, and they reminded me of dying stars. Why was he staring at me so intently? I wasn't the interesting one here. Ruadan was the half-fomoire demigod.

"Baleros has given me soldiers. Did you know that?" The red tip of Arubian's cigarette danced in the gloomy light as he gesticulated. "I can't say they've come in useful. They have been busy, after all, framing the Shadow Fae for their attacks. And they're protecting him in his palace. You'll never get past his army. You won't get within ten feet of him before they close in on you and blow you to pieces with iron shrapnel."

He blew another smoke ring into the air. "I might see if I can turn up to watch the show. Sometimes, I can feed off fae." Arubian shrugged. "I know fear. Know it as intimately as I do my own hands."

Of course the weirdo was intimate with his hands.

I took a step closer, waving the lantern. "Who are Burly Nan and whatever?"

A thin shrug from Arubian. "It doesn't matter if I tell you. You won't be in this world much longer, you know. Baleros gets more control every day. Fear is the easiest way to control humans. You were once their protectors. Not anymore. How quickly they're turning on you. Maybe you're immortals, but how long do you think you'll stay in your comfortable palace when the savage mob of millions turn on you? You'll be forced to wander the earth, tortured outcasts. I'll help them make the guillotines myself."

"Ciara, get your fire ready," I said. "Did you know it took humans an average of forty-five minutes to burn to death on medieval pyres? Our librarian told me that. Wonder what it takes for a fae."

For just a second, I saw fear flash in Arubian's eyes. So it *had* been good information.

Arubian's hand started shaking. "I see the hounds got you with their claws." He cocked his head. "You know, I could see death whispering around you when you fought," he said. "I'm very in tune with death."

Shit. I needed to shut him up.

And that's when Ruadan decided to reappear, solid as a brick building, right by my side. *Now* this conversation had his full interest.

I furrowed my brow, doing my best "get a load of this weirdo" face. "I have no idea what you're talking about," I said. "Death whispering around me? Sounds like some bad poetry."

He shook his head, eyes burning. "No. Not poetry. I feed off death fears. You instill them. I feel positively radiant around you."

My pulse started racing.

Ruadan took a step closer to him. "What are you talking about?"

"Surely you must see it," said Arubian. "She's not a normal fae."

"Is that all you have to tell me?" Ruadan's eyes slid to me. "She's not a normal fae. Anyone who meets … whatever her name is … can tell that right away."

So that's how it was. We'd gone from our romantic moment in the sewers to *whatever her name is.*

Arubian's smile was pure poison. "You want to know what she is, don't you? You want to know if you can trust her. Has her pretty body been confusing you, distracting you from the truth?"

"This is…" I sputtered, trying to block out the pain from my deep wounds so I could think clearly. "This is stupid. Honestly, are you going to listen to a man who spends his free time massacring people in his own personal roller disco? He's weird as shit." Every one of my muscles had tensed, my nerve endings igniting with a fight-or-flight instinct.

This is it. This is when they learn the truth.

CHAPTER 23

*A*rubian's orange eyes were on me. "You can't be more than a few decades old, but you instill death like an ancient being. If it hadn't been so delicious to feed from the fear you created in my hounds, I might be in a very bad mood indeed. As it is, I feel glorious. Perhaps we should spend more time together. We're alike, you and I."

"Fuck off." Why was it that the creepiest people kept telling me we were alike, like I was a long-lost sister to all the earth's monsters? I was going to develop a complex about it. "Who are Nan and Hal? Where's their gaff?"

Arubian cocked his head, his interest intense. A smile cracked his pale features. "Ahhh…. Can it really be?" He tapped his fingertips together, his features delighted. "Did *he* have a girl? I didn't know it was possible, and yet I see the evidence before me."

He *knew*. I had to stop him.

"Where is the house?" I demanded, my voice rising as I lost control. I tightened my grip on the lantern, panic cutting through my chest.

He pointed a long, bony finger at me. "Ruadan, I can tell you exactly who this one is. She's—"

The lantern was out of my hand before he could get another word out, the tip piercing his throat, ripping it open. Arubian fell back, his body slamming hard on the parquet floor. The pole had impaled his neck, ripping his vocal cords apart. As an ancient fae, the steel wouldn't kill him, but I'd managed to silence him for now.

A cold sweat rose on my skin, my heart hammering. We hadn't finished interrogating Arubian, and I'd completely screwed up the mission. Still, it wasn't like I'd had a choice. Arubian had nearly told the truth about me.

I stared at his body. Shock held me still for a moment as I tried to process what had just happened. The jagged wounds all around my torso ached, and I gripped my bleeding side. My heart was pumping hard, and blood poured from my neck, my sides—the claw and teeth marks all over my body. The damned shifters had shredded me to ribbons. With the pain and the shock roiling in my mind, it took me a moment to realize that Aengus was yelling at me.

"What the hells was that?" he was shouting. "We still don't know where Baleros is. You killed our only source of information before we'd got any real answers—all so you could hide the truth from us."

Nausea curdled my gut. The silence that fell was cold and damp as wet soil. I racked my mind to think of an explanation.

This did not look good for me. It was clear, now, that I had a secret I'd be willing to do almost anything to keep, and that didn't exactly mark me as trustworthy. Ruadan's eyes had shifted to black, and he was looking at me like I was his enemy.

Blocking out the pain from my wounds, I folded my arms, my gaze darting between the two Knights of the Shadow Fae.

"Arubian was wasting our time. He told us where to find Baleros. Nan and Burly Hal's place. We need to go now. Can you please open the portal?"

Aengus took a step closer, fury etched in his features. "Who the fuck are Nan and Burly Hal? Do you happen to know?"

"I thought you'd know." It sounded lame, even to me. I shot Ciara a pointed look, one that I hoped conveyed *help me here.*

"Yeah. Nan and Burly Hal," she added. "I've heard of them. Hackney, maybe? Or Islington by the tube station, near that kebab place?" She was terrible at bluffing.

Aengus growled, canines flashing. "This was all for nothing. All we've learned is that we're working with someone we can't trust at all. No—scratch that. We already knew that, considering you stabbed our Grand Master and left him to bleed. All you've done is confirm that you can't be trusted. Can we get rid of her now?"

My chest clenched. Our fragile alliance was falling apart fast.

Ruadan had gone so still, so quiet, it sent a cold thread of fear wending through my body. I could hardly see him, now, his body blending into the night. When I'd first met him, he'd seemed so ephemeral—a fleeting night wind, whispering over my skin. Then, I'd come to know him well enough that his violet eyes stood out like a neon sign to me, even when he was in his Wraith mode. But right now, he seemed to be slipping away from me, shadows blending into darkness. I couldn't see him anymore, couldn't grasp him. It seemed like there was something intentional about it.

The thought of losing him so fast opened a hollow pit in my chest.

I didn't even see Ruadan as he moved for me, had no idea where he was until I felt his finger on my arm, his touch feather-light. He leaned down to whisper in my ear so that only I could hear him. "This looks bad. And I don't know why, but I trust you implicitly and completely."

His words warmed me from the inside out. I wanted to throw my arms around him, but I knew it would look bad in front of Aengus. In fact, if Aengus saw us embracing, he'd assume Ruadan's mind was clouded by lust.

Was it?

Guilt twisted through me. I was hiding something important from Ruadan, and it should be obvious to him, now. I'd ruined the mission just to keep my secret.

"Of course you can trust me." The words tasted bitter in my mouth.

"What the hells is going on? Is she working with Baleros?" barked Aengus.

"Gods below, Aengus," I protested. "You have to know that I want him dead. I want him dead, and I want us to stay alive. That's what matters, isn't it?" This, at least, was the truth.

"She's telling the truth." Ruadan's tone brooked no argument. "I know she is."

At that moment, mist began pooling around us, and a shiver rippled up my spine. It whirled in unnatural eddies.

"Looks like Arubian's mist soldiers are finally arriving. We're out of time here."

Without another word, Ruadan turned and walked away. A sharp tendril of pain wound through me as he did. He trusted me for now, but he'd learn the truth at some point. And when he did, the trust would dissolve. We'd be enemies.

As he started speaking in Angelic, the parquet floor began rumbling.

All around us, the mist army materialized, fog twisting around their weapons. Then, from the shadows, the jackdaws began moving, running for us.

"We need to go *now*," I said.

Cracks began to widen in the ground, sparkly water gleaming in the chasms.

My heart skipped a beat at the sight of a jackdaw running for us at full speed. My jaw dropped at the sight of the bomb strapped to his waist.

"Jump!" I yelled. "Now!"

Ciara jumped in, then Aengus.

The blast went off, searing the skin on my right side just as Ruadan was pulling me in. The icy water soothed my burnt skin. As soon as we drifted deeper, Ruadan let go of my wrist.

I sank into the dark water. I hadn't felt this alone since Baleros had first thrown me in an empty, underground cage.

* * *

THE MISSION HAD BEEN a complete disaster, one that made me look as if I were working against the Institute. Why would Ruadan still trust me at this point?

Lungs burning, body burned and ripped, I climbed out of the portal. I was surprised to find that Ruadan had opened the portal into his own bedroom.

As I climbed out onto his flagstone floor, blood poured off my body. I flopped onto my back next to the portal, gasping for breath, wincing at my injuries. My mind whirled, the floor seeming to tilt beneath my back. I was in rough shape here.

From the floor, I heard Ruadan issue an order—Aengus was supposed to get Ciara settled in somewhere, an upgrade from her home under a car.

I gritted my teeth, closing my eyes. Did I even have any skin left on the right side of my body?

Gentle hands pulled my backpack from me, slipping off

the straps of my bug-out bag. A powerful pair of arms scooped me up, and I opened my eyes to look up at Ruadan.

"Sorry," I said.

"For lying?"

My throat tightened. "Sorry for killing Arubian prematurely."

He lay me down on the bed, and I grimaced.

"My skin hurts."

"Shhhh."

My eyes closed again, and I felt Ruadan's magic skimming over me, his fingertips tracing lightly around the ragged neck wound before moving down toward my side. Sleep was threatening to overwhelm me, but I fought to stay awake.

"You haven't told me everything, either," I said defensively. "You didn't tell me you were fomoire."

"Shhhh. Rest."

"You haven't told me what you feed off of."

His magic wrapped around me like a caress. "We only have fifteen hours," he said. "We'll address our precise natures after we kill Baleros."

He was right, of course, but I could tell that the distance between us bothered him as much as it bothered me. He wasn't meeting my eyes as he worked. I reached up and touched his cheek, and for just a moment, his gaze slid to me. I'd never seen him look so vulnerable before. Then, the spell was broken, and he ripped his attention away, concentrating completely on the claw marks on my side and the burns.

His magic was like a divine silk over my body. Still, I couldn't quite relax.

You and I are the same.

Blood still covered my skin, and my little roller disco clothes were sticking to me. I wanted those clothes off me before I fell asleep.

I forced my eyes open and pushed myself up onto my elbows. "I'm not going to sleep covered in blood," I muttered.

"You need rest."

I wasn't a monster. I didn't want to look like one. "I'll just be a minute. Don't go anywhere."

Half asleep, I stumbled to my feet and began peeling off my bloodied clothes, discarding them on Ruadan's bare floor. I crossed into the bathroom, where his bath of hot, bubbling spring water called to me. I slipped into it, my mind racing with images: death spreading out from my body like a miasma; Ruadan as a boy, threading a wreath of wildflowers for a mum who wouldn't wear them. After a minute, I stepped out of the tub and toweled off.

Wearing only a towel, I crossed back into his room.

I found the room empty, and my heart clenched. I couldn't explain it, but closeness to him was starting to feel like some basic, primal drive, as instinctive as the need to eat or sleep. I had a brief, overwhelming urge to run naked through the halls until I could find him and drag him back here and wrap my naked body around his, to force his lips to mine.

Tears stung my eyes. I'd let these fantasies trail on far enough. We could never be together, and there was no point obsessing over it. Morning sunlight streamed in through the window.

The survival instinct in me told me what I needed now more than anything else: sleep.

I crawled into Ruadan's bed and pulled the covers up around me, slipping fast into a dreamless sleep.

CHAPTER 24

I awoke to the tawny evening sun.

I had the strangest feeling that a boom had sounded, but I couldn't tell if it had been in my dream or real life. In fact, considering I'd been healed and rested, I felt oddly delirious. I blinked, trying to clear my mind, but the edges of everything around me seemed hazy.

"Ruadan," I whispered.

It took me a moment to realize the bed was empty. Where had Ruadan gone? And why was the world tilting back and forth like I was on a boat?

My mouth felt like cotton, and I licked my lips, trying to get up to speed mentally.

Let's see … roller disco, hounds…. Oh, and we had a time limit before Baleros unleashed the Black Death and told everyone I was Adonis's daughter. And I'd just spent many hours sleeping. Why hadn't anyone woken me? And what the hells was wrong with my head?

I rolled to my side. Plaster and stone dust covered the sheets. What the hells?

BOOM. The walls shook, and more dust rained down on top of me, the bed trembling.

What in the world was going on?

I sat bolt upright. When the sheets fell off me, I realized I was still naked. My clothes from yesterday still lay on the floor—shredded, wet, and blood-soaked. Every other time I'd woken in the Institute, I'd found fresh clothes left by someone or other, and the room tidied.

Dizzy, I rose and crossed to Ruadan's dresser. Off-balance, I stumbled, then rested for a moment on the wood. I pulled on my underwear and boots, but the rest of my clothes had been shredded the night before.

I pulled a drawer open, then picked out one of Ruadan's shirts—a black one with buttons. I pulled it on, and the hem reached halfway down my thighs.

What time was it? Surely, we only had a few hours left. I should never have slept so long. What was I doing? Confusion clouded my mind.

BOOM!

My heart shuddered. Were we under attack? Off-balance, I crossed to the windows. I touched the glass, staring outside. From here, I had a view of the courtyard and the inner ring of connected towers. Somewhere beyond the outer wall, dark smoke curled into the air. I sniffed—gasoline and a strong chemical scent floated on the wind, along with burning wood and stone. Jackdaws bombing us again?

My limbs were too heavy. I looked down at my wrists. For just a moment, I caught the faint shimmer of magic pulsing through my veins. Something was happening to me.

Frantically, I snatched my bug-out bag off the floor. It had almost dried after the last trip through the portal. As I stumbled, I shoved my hand into the bag, picking out a soggy Galaxy chocolate bar. My stomach rumbled, and I tore it open as I walked, gnawing into it.

I pushed through the door into the courtyard, squinting at the blazing afternoon light. The sun dazzled me, and I shielded my eyes with my arm.

BOOM.

Instinctively, I ducked, covering my head as the earth shook. From inside the fortress walls, I still couldn't see a damn thing—just the smoke rising above the towers.

Then, I forced myself up, holding out my arms to steady myself. I broke into a jog, rushing into the Cailleach Tower.

As I moved, voices whispered around me. The colors seemed too bright today—garish, almost.

In the Tower, I gripped the banister hard to get myself up the stairs.

At last, I reached the throne room.

Melusine was on the floor, hunched over a book, with a tall stack of volumes by her side. Aengus sat slumped against one of the columns. He looked dazed, his jaw slack. His mouth opened and closed mutely. What was he doing just sitting there?

"What's happening?" I swayed on my feet. "I don't feel right. And you don't look right."

Aengus stared at the ground. "Poi—poi … porcu-pie."

"Poison," said Melusine. "We think. I'm amazed you're up at all. Aengus isn't doing so well."

"Poison from what?" Was it connected to the bombs blowing up our Tower?

"I've been working on it for hours," said Melusine from the floor. "Aengus and Ruadan have both been delirious all day, though Aengus took a sharp turn for the worse about an hour ago."

"And you're fine?" I slurred.

She nodded. "We think it came from Arubian's palace. At least, that's what I think. Ruadan and Aengus aren't doing much thinking at all."

I glanced at Aengus again. For just a moment, a vicious look in his eyes sent ice through my blood, and his face seemed to transform, dark veins streaking his skin. Then, his jaw went slack again, eyes unfocused. My blood surged.

Was I hallucinating?

Focus. "Where is everyone?"

"All the other knights are still out searching for Baleros. Searching for something to do with Nan and Hal. Quite frankly, we don't really know what we're doing right now."

"Don't trust," said Aengus. "Don't trust Arianna. Parry … honor…."

My lip curled, fingers tightening into fists. *I come from the Horseman of Death, and I will end you.* Aengus was making me angry, using what seemed to be the last of his dwindling brain power to cast doubt on me. I wanted to shut him up.

Aengus managed to point at me. "Who … are your parents?"

The death instinct swooped through my skull, threatening to erupt. Phantom wings tingled on my shoulder blades. *It's time to let you know the truth about myself.* I lunged for Aengus, then slammed my fist hard into his jaw.

I reared back my hand to hit him again, but a piercing scream stopped me.

I whirled to find Melusine staring at us, gripping the book. "Stop! Both of you!" she shouted. "Look, I see two people under the effects of the poison getting angry, I think maybe the poison is at fault. That's just me."

I unclenched my fist, still staring at Aengus. Guilt flooded me. The guy was near death, and I'd just bashed him in the skull.

"Sorry," I muttered. "I'm not thinking. I'm sorry. Sorry. Sorry." I couldn't stop saying the word.

"Shhhh," said Melusine. "Just stay away from him. You two both need to keep a distance."

Melusine was talking sense, as usual.

"Right," I conceded. "Where is Ruadan? Out searching with the other knights?"

She flipped a page in the book, and the gesture looked angry. I'd annoyed her. "No, Ruadan and Aengus never made it out, because of the poison. Ruadan is doing better than Aengus, on account of Ruadan being a demigod and Aengus being just your average, everyday, run-of-the-mill fae." She cocked her head. "Doesn't explain why you're doing better than Aengus. I guess we'll get to that later. Right now, we have to stop Aengus from dying, because the poison is eating his brain at an alarming rate. Ruadan and his mum went outside to try to kill humans."

"That doesn't sound good," I drawled. "And the booms?"

Melusine cleared her throat. "Humans have made makeshift nail bombs. Full of scraps of iron that can kill fae. They're lobbing them through the hole in the moat."

My skin grew cold, and my mind cleared for a moment. "Ruadan is out there, delirious, in the middle of nail bombs?"

Melusine shrugged. "Queen Macha is with him, feeding off their deaths."

I pinched the bridge of my nose. I needed to caution them about something—there was an added danger there, if I could just put my finger on it. Thoughts wafted through my mind like dandelion seeds in the wind, and I reached out to snatch one.

"Wait. Wait. Arubian was right. If the humans see Ruadan killing them, they'll turn on us. We can't fight them all. This is bad PR. Very bad."

Even in my fog of confusion, I was beginning to understand that we were screwed. We had only a few hours left till the Plague hit. Humans were attacking us. Oh, and we'd been poisoned.

Baleros was about to win again—because, of course, he always did.

Aengus's skin was shot through with dark veins once more, and his head lolled. Just moments ago, I had been ready to batter him to death. Now, panic gripped me at the sight of him withering before my eyes. The only one still functioning here was Melusine.

"What have you found in your books?" I demanded.

She scratched her cheek. "I found in the literature references to a legendary unicorn named Nan. That's about it."

I winced. "I don't suppose the unicorn is a promising lead?"

"No." She pulled out another book. "And I haven't been able to spend long on that. I'm trying to figure out the poisons first. One thing at a time, you know what I mean?" She cracked the book open.

Whispers sounded around my head, breath on my neck. I leaned against a column to steady myself, and dread tightened my chest. "We're running out of time." I had a bad feeling that as time dwindled, Ruadan would simply give himself over to Baleros. He'd stand in front of the gate in iron cuffs.

I bit my lip hard. I shouldn't have killed Arubian so fast.

From the floor, Aengus was trying to say the word "unicorn."

I crossed my arms, gripping my own biceps hard to try to clear my thoughts.

Nan ... Nan ... Nan....

Queen Nan....

The pain of my own grip helped me clear my head a little to think. There was something familiar about the name Nan, if I could only grasp onto it.

Nan ... Queen Nan's lace....

"I know the name Nan." I started pacing, closing my eyes.

"You should have woken me up earlier. I could have figured this out."

I was mentally ticking over the name Nan. It was such a plain, solid, unsexy name, that it had stuck in my brain....

"Nan," I said at last. "Nan Bullen."

Melusine looked up from her book. "Who?"

"The demoness queen I saved from one of the hell worlds. Her name is Nan Bullen. Queen. She lives in one of the empty rooms here. Didn't know what else to do with her after I saved her." Melusine and Aengus just stared at me as I swayed on my feet. "It's worth a shot, isn't it?"

CHAPTER 25

Dressed in her green gown, Queen Nan Bullen swanned into the throne room, a golden crown gleaming on her dark hair. In her six-fingered hand, she held a long, thin cigarette.

She took a puff, the smoke curling around her. "You called for a queen?"

Might as well get right to the point. "Do the names Nan and Burly Hal mean anything to you?"

She strode up to the empty throne like she owned it, then draped herself in the chair, letting her legs dangle over the edge. She chuckled darkly. "Nan and Burly Hal. How could you not know? Forgotten so quickly, time fleeth before us like a hind through the wood."

Oh, please get to the point. I wasn't sure I could keep myself standing much longer.

It was at that point that Ruadan strode into the room, his dark clothing glistening with blood. He looked a lot steadier than I felt, but his eyes were pure black.

"Who is this?" he asked.

"This is Queen Nan," I slurred. "Did you fix the problem outside?"

"No."

The queen cocked her head at Ruadan, smiling coquettishly. "Have you come to praise my beauty? I'll accept a poem."

Dark magic whirled around her, and in it, I saw wolves and stags forming. She tapped her cigarette holder, and ash dropped onto the floor in a neat little pile before the throne.

Ruadan's magic iced the room. "Do you know who Burly Hal is?"

Queen Nan's sigh was a delicate thing. "Do you know I didn't even feel it when they cut off my head? He brought in a French swordsman. That, at least, was a nice gesture. If I'd made a spectacle of myself like the Countess of Salisbury, running around with chunks out of my flesh as the axeman chased me, I'd have never lived it down in my hell world. Not that they gave me much respect, anyway." She pointed at a tall, peaked window. "My death spot was just over there. My blood stained the stones, dripping through the wooden scaffold. Noble blood, not that it spared my life."

At last, even with the fog in my mind, I started to piece it together.

And apparently, Ruadan had, too, because he said, "Queen Anne Boleyn."

She lifted her hand. "Didn't have six fingers when I was alive. The gods gave me an extra one in the hell world. Bastards."

She looked at me, her dark eyes enchanting.

"You want Burly Hal? He was my husband, Henry VIII. You killed his demon form in the hell world. Thank you for that. He was a deeply unpleasant person."

"What was the home built for you?" Ruadan was rubbing a knot in his forehead. "We need to know, now."

Another delicate sigh. "He had the whole place engraved with our initials, intertwined. True love, it was. Until he moved on—"

"The home," Ruadan barked. "A palace?"

Those dandelion seeds of thoughts wafted through my mind…. A Tudor palace … pearls and silk.

I scowled at Ruadan. "Weren't you alive when it was built? You should know this."

"I hardly paid attention to human affairs," he shot back. "Humans are alive one instant and dead the next. There's not much point in learning their names."

"Quite true in my case," said Nan, her smile electrifying. She seemed to be enjoying the attention so much, I had a feeling she wouldn't let it escape her grasp so quickly. She'd cling to it like a drowning woman clung to a branch. "I'll accept a love poem as payment."

I glanced at Melusine, who was still flipping furiously through a book about poison.

Ruadan stared at Nan, his whole body tensed, a lion about to strike. I had the impression he was fighting his natural impulse to simply attack and terrify her until she gave him what he wanted, but some gentlemanly part of him reined it in. He stood there, shadows cutting the air around him.

"He'd be really bad at poetry even on the best of days. No good," I said. "He barely speaks, and when he does, it's usually about death. But he has the nicest muscles." I giggled.

Shit. Had I said that out loud?

Nan blinked her long eyelashes. "A song, then, from the muscled gentleman! Compose me a song, dedicated to my beauty."

"It's not going to happen," I shouted, losing patience. "If you want romance, Aengus can sort of paw at you. He's lonely and he has soft hands since he never worked a real day in his life."

She flashed me a look of pure, hot rage. Right. So it wasn't lust she was after, but actual courtly love or whatever. Something I honestly didn't understand.

I turned to Ruadan, grabbing his arm. "Can you make her one of your floral wreaths?"

Ruadan cut me a sharp look, and I knew he was still considering violence. He'd be producing neither a crown, nor a poem, nor a song. See, men never had to be flexible in that way. He could just stand there, rigid as a rock, and say *this is who I am, and I'll be fucked if I'm changing.* Women—like me and Queen Nan here—we were used to being mutable. I could be flirtatious when the situation called for it, or aggressive when I needed someone to fear me. I could be funny or flattering, or I could take charge. I didn't necessarily do it all well, but I was used to adapting.

Perhaps I had to field this one.

I stepped forward, struggling to keep my balance.

"Beautiful queen." I stumbled over my words. "Your beauty is like a moon, and also like jewels, and like … dew on the grass. And your eyes are like—" I let out a long breath. "A lovely pair of beetles. No. Those dark volcanic stones, and like the black heart at the center of Queen Nan's lace. Cheeks like … pink flowery petals made of skin." I winced. "Breasts like two fleshy flotation devices."

Well, I'd done my best.

She nodded, satisfied. "Fair enough. Hampton Court—"

"Hampton Court Palace!" Melusine shouted, hand raised. "I just remembered."

"Thanks Melusine," I said. "Very helpful."

Queen Nan leaned back in the throne. "It's not fortified like this place is. No tower walls to keep it in. Has your enemy got a powerful army, by any chance, to defend him?"

"Yes," I sighed. Somehow, Queen Nan had become part of our strategic planning process, since she was one of the few here who could think straight. "And we haven't got an army."

"I'll go into the palace on my own," said Ruadan. "I'm leaving now."

"How?" I asked. "Night hasn't fully fallen yet. You won't be able to shadow-leap around."

"I can create night." He looked dazed. "We can't waste any more time."

"Wait." My jaw dropped. "You can *create night?*"

A flicker of night darkness swirled around his powerful body. "It's a temporary, artificial night. The sun seems to disappear, the stars come out." Ruadan scrubbed his hand over his jaw, eyes on the floor as he thought. "But the only problem is … the only problem is…."

Ruadan was struggling to finish his thought. I, too, understood there was something wrong with this plan, but I couldn't put my finger on it.

Melusine raised her hand. "It would instantly alert Baleros that you were there."

BOOM. The walls shook. Apparently, the humans weren't done hurling their grenades at us. I held onto a column to stabilize myself, woozy as hell.

"Not to mention," Melusine added, "you've all been poisoned. Am I right? You wouldn't be able to create night that easily."

Ruadan paced the room, not answering. "Night will fall in two and a half hours," he eventually said. "That leaves us only a half hour after darkness falls…." His dark gaze went unfocused again.

Three hours left. When I closed my eyes, my mind filled with images of rotting bodies in the street. I gasped, opening my eyes again.

I bit my lip hard to clear my thoughts, then began pacing furiously across the floor. "You can't attack him like this.

Even if we find the palace, you'll be dead within moments unless you're completely sharp. He'll be ready for you," I muttered.

"We have to be prepared for the fact that Adonis might be there," said Ruadan.

I closed my eyes, and my father's image flashed in my mind like a lightning bolt. Blue eyes, golden skin, black hair. Once we achieved our objectives—once Ruadan killed Baleros, my father was next on his list. Then me. Would this happen tonight?

At every moment, I was moving closer to the execution block—my father and me, moving up together. My blood would drip through the scaffold onto the stones below.

Not if I got the mist army first. Whoever killed Baleros got his army. Ruadan had said he needed the immortal army to kill Adonis. Maybe he needed it to kill me, too.

I bit my lip so hard I pierced the skin. Blood pooled in my mouth, and I forced those thoughts out of my mind.

I had to go with him. I had to kill Baleros before he did.

"I'll go with you," I blurted. "Once darkness falls completely, you can distill your Wraith magic. That thing that makes it so hard to see you. Give me that, too." I held up a hand, wiggling my fingers. "Look. You can put it in a ring, and I'll slip in with you. I can wear the lumen crystal. I'll zoom around the palace, all silent, until I find him. Until I find Adonis." I shook my head. *Not Adonis.* "Baleros. Until I find Baleros."

Ruadan was rubbing his forehead again. "I need to be the one to kill Baleros. I need to restrain him and take him through the portal. Only I can do that. I just can't think…."

BOOM.

I gritted my teeth at the explosion. The humans were really starting to piss me off at this point.

"I'll send ravens out," said Ruadan. "They'll swoop over

Hampton Court Palace now, and they'll report back if anything seems unusual. Fortifications, guards, weapons, anything. In the meantime, I'm calling back all the knights from the search for Baleros. We need them on top of every gate, patrolling every outer wall."

"Except we can't just kill them," I said. What would Baleros do? "We need the humans on our side. Create a tyrant."

Ruadan's lip twitched. "One who oppresses the masses."

"Execute him publicly," I added.

"I'm afraid I'm a bit lost here," said Melusine. "Anyone care to fill me in?"

"Turning the tables on Baleros," said Ruadan. "Framing him for the killing we're about to do."

"Fighting back against the humans while making it clear Baleros is behind all this," I said. "Let them think he's in power here."

Melusine frowned. "And how are we supposed to convince Londoners that Baleros has taken over the Institute within the next few hours?"

"We fly his flag over the tower," said Ruadan. "Create the impression that he's invaded."

Aengus groaned from the floor. "My head. My head. Headddd."

Oh, right. Aengus was about to die from poison. "Have you found anything useful yet, Melusine?" I snapped. "We're about to lose one of our knights here."

"Give me a minute," shouted Melusine, flipping another page. "It's not as simple as— Oh, hang on. This is it! The poison. It's from Arubian's hounds. All you need is a skilled fae mage to reverse it, one who knows potions from the Old Gods. If you don't, it says here in the literature that immediate death follows a period of delirium and decreasing mental acuity. The brain literally turns to liquid. So that's unpleasant."

Shit.

"Good," said Ruadan, absentmindedly. "But we have no mages skilled in the magic of the Old Gods. Not since Esther got into a fight with the gorta and starved to death in the grass moat."

"Kill me," said Aengus weakly.

Mum. My mother had known the magic of the Old Gods. She'd know what to do.

If only I'd paid attention to her lessons before she died….

CHAPTER 26

I swallowed hard, tiredness creeping up on me, stirring up my thoughts. My mother had known about the Old Gods—she'd known all about them. *She'd* be able to cure us all. A dark laugh escaped me, echoing off the stone.

My father had killed the person who could save us now.

My confusion had sharp edges, a dark delirium. I'd died once. Iron sword right through my heart. I'd drifted into the afterworld, and my father had caught me. I clamped my eyes shut, the possibilities swarming in my mind.

Would Adonis be there tonight when we invaded Hampton Court Palace? Would I find my father again?

My shoulders had tensed so much they hurt. When I closed my eyelids, I saw my father's face again: his golden skin, the gray-blue eyes. I never knew him as the Angel of Death—not until the end. I knew him as the man who brought me warm milk at night and read me Greek myths in bed by candlelight.

I'd see him soon, wouldn't I? I felt his presence around

CRAWFORD C.N.

me, and his rich scent of myrrh, the warmth of his hug. A phantom angel feather brushed my cheek.

That day, when Ruadan had invaded, my father had lost control. He'd killed everyone with his fear, waves of death rippling out from his body.

What had the shock done to him once he realized he'd killed my mum? When he'd seen her bleeding from the mouth? What if the trauma had warped him, turning him into a vengeful creature—one who wanted to spread death? One who'd be willing to work with Baleros?

The whispers grew louder around me, and now, I could hear what they were saying. They were repeating Ruadan's thoughts.

Creatures like you were never meant to walk the earth.

Pivoting, I turned to pace the floor again. I wasn't a proper horseman of death like my father was. I didn't have the power that he did. I'd killed a few fae when they'd ganged up on me, but that was it. Only Adonis—Thanatos himself— could slaughter an entire city at once.

I couldn't do that. I wasn't like him. I wasn't a monster.

When I opened my eyes again, I realized I was gripping my own hair, and Ruadan was staring at me.

"Something weighing heavily on your soul?" asked Ruadan.

"No," I said sharply. "It's just the poison. And I don't know a mage skilled in the powers of the Old Gods."

"I know of one," said Ruadan. "But she doesn't trust men anymore, and she's unlikely to help me. How much time do we have, Melusine?"

"It says here that once language abilities deteriorate, uhh … you got about a half hour before Aengus kicks it," she replied. "Maybe a bit more."

I sucked in a sharp breath. We couldn't let Aengus die.

178

"Lead me to this woman, Ruadan. We'll go together. I'll do my best to charm her."

Ruadan nodded. "Fine. I'll summon the other knights to secure the fortress. Melusine, you make Baleros's flag. A bundle of sticks. Raise it as soon as you can. I'll try to get the antidote, along with Arianna or whatever her name is."

"Bunch of sticks with an axe blade." Melusine pushed up her glasses. "I know. You don't worry about a thing, Grand Master Ruadan. I'll get the flag flying faster than you can say … an epic poem of some kind. Something that would take about twenty-three minutes to say. In other words, it will take about twenty-three minutes for me to make it."

BOOM.

I clamped my hands over my ears. Was it the delirium, or were these explosions growing louder?

"Where exactly are we going?" I asked as the ground rumbled beneath my feet.

The World Key at Ruadan's neck glowed, and dark magic snapped around him. "Emain."

The floor cracked and opened up under me, and I plunged into the cold water.

* * *

AN HOUR *and thirty minutes left.*

I pulled myself up out of the portal, and freezing water poured from my body onto damp, mossy soil. Ruadan was already standing in the forest. Oak boughs arched over him, and the air smelled heavy with earth and musk and … apples? I breathed in again, closing my eyes. This was the land of my dreams.

I still felt confused, but here, the delirium had taken on a lighter feel, no longer as dark and sharp.

Ruadan nodded, his black clothing sculpting his perfect

179

body, pale hair down his back. I pulled myself out and stood, my body dripping water.

Ruadan had gone still, tuning into something. It took me a moment to hear the distant sound of drums trembling over the earth.

"Why do those drums sound familiar?" I asked.

"Because you heard them in one of my memories. It's the Wrenne Festival. The night of the sacred hunt." Late sunlight sparkled through the tree branches, and Ruadan squinted in the honeyed light. "Nyxobas, god of night, will be covering this land at any moment, turning day into night. He draws down night, here, because he is worshiped."

"What do you mean?"

"I mean night will fall any moment here, just for the festival. Nyxobas does that."

"Could you call in a favor with your granddad and ask him to kill Baleros on our behalf?"

"He doesn't do favors like that. He doesn't care if I live or die. He only cares if he's worshiped."

I blinked. "He sounds charming." I twisted the hem of my dress, wringing out the cold water onto the earth. "Where's this friend of yours who hates men?"

"She'll be at the festival." When I looked up, I realized how close I was standing to Ruadan. I let myself indulge for a moment in breathing in his piney scent. We could just stay here….

"I don't want the queen to know that we're here," Ruadan added.

Oh, right. The mission. "Any reason?"

"My sister will want a formal audience. She'll want to know about our mother, what condition she's in, what's happened to her. Why we've been poisoned. She'll want to know what my plans are, what my mother's plans are, how

I'll capture Baleros, and so on. It will take hours that we don't have."

"How do we stay hidden?"

Ruadan stroked a hand down his chest. "Wrenne is a festival of disguises. We dress ourselves from the bounty of the forest and hide our faces."

"So what exactly do we wear? Leaves?"

"Hemlock boughs, oak leaves, animal skins, furs, antlers."

Was this his confusion, or did he really think we were about to rustle up some animal skins and antlers right now?

I looked up at the sun slanting lower on the horizon. Mauve and pumpkin stained a sapphire sky—Nyxobas's unnatural sunset, starting already.

I toyed with the fabric of my wet dress. Once again, I seemed to have moved closer to Ruadan, as if drawn by an invisible thread. Now, I was only inches from him, and I felt an electrical pulse moving between us. My eyes lingered over his lips, and I remembered how it had felt when he'd pressed them against mine, how my body had lit up when he'd touched me.

"I'm getting distracted," I muttered.

"Wrenne does that to people. Not to mention, our minds…." He trailed off. He'd gone completely still, but his magic pulsed onto my body, hot strokes up my neck, up my thighs.

I could have sworn I felt his magic licking between my legs, and I gasped. Was he doing that on purpose?

"We don't have a lot of time," he added. His voice stroked over my skin, an intoxicating caress.

Still, he wasn't moving, and his eyes pierced me, taking me apart piece by piece.

What had I said to him after our moment in the sewer? That it had been a mistake, and it could never happen again.

I'd already let myself get deep enough into this. I'd let myself care too much.

"Like you said." My voice came out husky. "We have a time limit. Pressed for time."

His eyes stayed locked on me as if he were mesmerized. "The drums."

"The drums," I repeated. I could feel their rhythm pulsing through my blood like a heartbeat. I forced myself to step back from Ruadan, and I glanced at the sky again. "We need that antidote."

Between the leaves, the mauve hues had deepened to a dark blue, and the moon seemed to hang over us. I could still feel Ruadan's heat radiating around me, his magic tingling over my skin.

When I looked down from the darkening sky, Ruadan had disappeared, and I was completely on my own.

I was utterly losing it. "Ruadan?"

CHAPTER 27

*I*t took a minute before he answered.

Then, at last, his voice floated from the shadows: "You need a disguise."

I took a deep breath, then bit my lip again to master my thoughts. I understood dressing like a human, wearing the appropriate outfits for nightclubs and bars, but clothing myself in leaves was a bit unfamiliar.

I crossed to an oak, its trunk wrapped with ivy, and pulled a knife from my thigh holster. I cut through the ropes of vines until I'd formed a large pile of them on the earth.

Then, I knelt on the ground and rifled through my bug-out bag until I found a plastic mini stapler. I smiled. How anyone got through life without a bug-out bag was beyond me.

I stood and began stripping off my clothes, starting with my wet shirt. The crisp forest air slid over my bare skin as I pulled off my bra, and my breasts peaked in the breeze. I slid off my knickers next. For just a moment, I lingered there, thinking of Ruadan, wishing he'd come back.

Focus on the mission.

I crouched, naked, on the earth. The forest breeze whispered over my bare skin, raising goosebumps. My mind turned back to Ruadan's delicious magic, his mouth. I had to stop myself from hunting him down right now. Licking my lips, I shoved the shirt, my underwear, and my boots into the bag.

With the drums pounding in my belly, I wasn't sure I could keep my hands off Ruadan. Even without him here, liquid desire was lighting me up. I lifted the ivy off the ground and stood.

Focus, Liora. We're here on a mission. Put on your damn leaf clothes.

I clenched my jaw, forcing my attention to the ivy. I began wrapping it around myself, and it skimmed over my skin, the leaves soft as silk. I stapled the leaves and stems together over my chest. Then, I tied the vines around my lower half, creating a short shirt.

When I'd just about covered up my bum, I turned to find Ruadan staring at me. "How long have you been standing there?"

Given the darkness in his eyes, I was guessing he'd been there for a while. He didn't speak, reverting into his eerie animal stillness, and the forest wind whisked over us.

His chest was bare, now, and he wore a kilt of animal skins and a pair of antlers. A cluster of leaves covered the World Key at his throat.

"Where did you get all that?" I asked.

His dark gaze drank me in, sliding slowly down my breasts, my bare waist, my hips….

Then, abruptly, he turned to the oak next to him. He ripped a bunch of leaves from a bough. Frowning, he worked at them for a minute until he'd created two masks of oak leaves, each with eye holes and a strap around the back, made of the stems.

That was … impressive.

He handed me one of the masks, and I slid it over my head, smiling at him.

Then, I snatched my bag from the ground, slipping it over my shoulders.

We started walking in step, moving to the rhythm of the drum. The setting sunlight streamed through the tree branches, and night began to claim Emain's forest.

Ahead of us, someone raced through the oaks: a woman wearing a scrap of animal skin, flowers over her breasts. She wore a floral wreath on her head, and ribbons streamed behind her, tangled in her ginger hair. Just a few paces behind her, a man ran past, antlers on his head.

I frowned. "So is this basically a festival where men wear antlers and chase women around in the woods and try to have sex with them?"

"Yes."

Well, there it was. It was remarkably similar to what Uncle Darrell and his humans attempted in Richmond Park, except I assumed in Emain people here actually got laid. "And that's it?"

"Sometimes the women chase the men," he added. "There are bonfires, music. We sacrifice sixteen prisoners in a bonfire, and we eat things made with apples, like pies—"

"Wait," I held up a hand. "Did you just slip in a bit about burning people to death?"

"The prisoners, yes. In the bonfire. Then we have pies made from—"

"I understand how pies work. That part doesn't need that much explaining. I'm stuck on the burning people to death part."

"Oh?"

"I mean, at the very least, don't the tormented screams of the damned kind of kill the sexy vibe you're all going for?"

He frowned, tracing a hand over his bare chest. "How so?"

My stomach dropped. "You know what? This is probably one of those things it's better if we don't talk about. Let's just chalk this up to a cultural difference, and we will not talk about it, because I'm starting to think problems between people are better when you don't talk about them." I might have been babbling a little.

"You should really sleep more."

I scowled at him. "It's the poison making me confused."

"In general, you should sleep more. In a bed, not on the floor."

"In *your* bed?"

A wicked smile, just for a moment. "Perhaps."

I liked Ruadan when he let down his guard. Too bad this couldn't last.

An enormous bonfire gleamed in a clearing in the distance, roaring at least six feet high. Maybe that was where we burned the prisoners. I *really* hoped we'd be missing that part of the evening.

This time, when I glanced at the sky, it had darkened to a midnight purple. The moon beamed over the tree line—unnaturally large—and the drums rumbled in my belly. I closed my eyes, breathing in the heavy air, its scent mossy and sweet at the same time. The atmosphere somehow felt fertile here. I stole another glance at Ruadan's bare chest.

You'd think that a man in an animal-skin skirt, a leaf mask, and deer antlers would look a *bit* off. It's not a look you're likely to find in men fashion's blogs or on *GQ*'s best-dressed list. But somehow, it looked perfect on Ruadan. He looked like he'd emerged from the forest itself, a man hewn from its oaks and rocks, driven by wild, animal instincts. I found myself licking my lips. It took me a moment to realize Ruadan was staring at me, too, his eyes blazing at the sight of my tongue lingering on my lower lip.

When we reached the clearing, I surveyed the space around us. Here, revelers were dancing around the bonfire. Bare-chested men wore masks made of animal skins and feathers, faces blank, featureless. They'd painted their bodies with white and blue symbols. Like me, many of the women wore nothing but leaves, so I didn't have to endure the *flaming forest fuck-party faux pas* of coming underdressed.

Across from me, a man in enormous antlers danced around the fire on oak stilts, his face covered in leather. Others wore what looked like burlap over their faces, the effect unnerving overall.

"Do you see her?" I asked in a loud whisper.

He sniffed the air, then shook his head. "She's not here yet."

"You know her by her smell?"

"Yes."

"How well do you know her, exactly? That you can just sniff the air and smell her body?"

Firelight danced over his masculine features, and he didn't answer. Classic Wraith move.

One of the masked dancers swooped closer to me, his head surrounded by raven feathers. The dancers were chanting something in the ancient fae language. Was it something about making sweet, sweet love to the sound of prisoners burning to death? It was anyone's guess.

The fire blazed hot, dry heat wavering over my skin. I was at least twelve feet away from it, but it still drew beads of sweat on my forehead and the tops of my breasts.

I leaned closer to Ruadan. "We don't have to join in the dancing, do we?"

"No." He nodded at the forest path. "But if we stand here, we'll draw attention to ourselves. We should wait in the cover of the trees until she arrives.

I was only too happy to move away from the creepy

masked dancers, and I stepped backward to the tree line. The fire heated my skin even from here.

The atmosphere intoxicated me, luring me away from my task. Thoughts flitted through my mind like fireflies. *Find the girl ... bring her back to the Institute ... kill Baleros....*

Worship Nyxobas ... worship the night ... hunt. Join the hunt here.

Death blooms in you like a seed. Make the most of life.

A few steps deeper into the forest's darkness, and it was just me and Ruadan. My body heated.

Worship the forest.

CHAPTER 28

*W*hen I looked at Ruadan, I felt certain no one else in the world existed. I smiled at him, chest flushing. The drums pounded louder in my ears, the rhythms reverberating over my skin. As I studied Ruadan's body—thickly corded, built to kill—heat swooped through my core.

The forest wanted me to enjoy myself.

My fingers slipped into the top of my leaf skirt, and I tugged it down. Why was I wearing this? The night didn't want me to wear this. The night forest wanted me naked— wanted my palms and knees in the earth, hips up, legs wide on the ground underneath him.

The hunt was calling to me. I took another step back into the bosom of the forest, and my bare feet sank into the rich soil. Ruadan's eyes were locked on me, and he prowled closer. His gaze took in my mouth, then lowered to the curves of breasts. My nipples tightened under his stare.

I wanted the leaves off me, wanted my knees in the dirt, wanted to gasp along with him. Wanted to breathe in his heat, his musk and salt. Wanted to fill myself…. I was *hungry*.

CRAWFORD C.N.

I ached with need. My teeth, my tongue, my mouth needed his body. My body needed his mouth, tongue on my thighs, between my legs.

Another step back into in the woods' embrace, and Ruadan was prowling after me, eyes gleaming with silver. He was a god of the hunt moving after his prey. I tugged down the leaves at my waist even more, showing him the curve of my hips. *This is what you need.* Ruadan's muscles tightened.

Lure him closer....

I turned away from him, facing a tree. I wanted to feel his fingers brushing between my legs, his hot mouth on my throat. My back arched, legs spreading in invitation.

It took only another heartbeat for Ruadan to find his way to me. His powerful body pressed against me, warming me. Then, he slid his hand over my belly, and he brushed it down slowly.

I want. I want. I want.

His fingers traced over the hollows of my hips. My back arched, hips grinding into him.

I felt the cold air skimming over my bare skin through the leaves. The drums were stoking something primal in me, something between a sex drive and bloodlust.

Get what you want.

I turned to face Ruadan, and I slid my hands up his chest, grazing my nails against his torso. I gripped his shoulders, then tried to push him to the ground. His enormous body didn't budge.

I pushed him hard in the chest. "On the ground."

I leapt on him, wrapping my legs around him, and he fell back to the earth.

With a coy smile, I leaned down. I straddled him, whispering in his ear. "I want you to see me. The *real* me." I wasn't quite sure what I was saying, but the words were just tumbling out.

190

He looked feral, canines flashing. How long would he let me be on top of him before he threw me to the earth and tried to dominate me? He gripped me hard by the waist, fingers possessive.

I pressed my mouth to his neck, giving him a little lick, a flick of my tongue over his skin. The hint of salt tasted delicious, and I rocked my hips over him. I licked again, reveling in the feel of his hands on me. I brushed light, sweet kisses over his throat, then moved lower over his collarbone, his chest.

His body was tense as a bow string, and with each kiss on his chest, I felt him twitch. His magic was skimming over me like silk, stroking my body in places I wanted to feel his hands.

I kissed him on the mouth again, rolling my hips into his. When I pulled away from the kiss, I caught his lower lip between my teeth.

He stroked a hand up into my hair, gripping it hard. The other hand was on my bum.

I kissed his neck slowly. I rocked my hips again, pleasure racing up my body from the apex of my thighs.

He reached for the leaves over my breasts, ready to tear them off.

I gripped his hand, stopping him. My body heated. "Wait."

I took in the perfect, masculine planes of his body, the scent of pine and apples. I ached for him so hard I could barely think of anything else. Still, I wanted something from him. I needed him to speak to me.

I leaned down, whispering in his ear. "I need you to tell me that you want me."

On top of Ruadan, I felt like a goddess. The intensity in his dark eyes made my body heat and swell. He was looking at me like he wanted to fling me to the ground—like he wanted to flip me over onto my hands and knees and claim me. He was resisting. Always resisting.

I tugged down the leaves just a little to reveal the swell of my breasts, and I moved my hips over him. "I want the truth from you. Say it to me."

"And what about your truth—?"

I clamped a hand over his mouth.

No. No. Not that. Not my truth.

My heart thundered. "I want to hear the truth about how you feel about me."

His eyes widened, swirling with black. I leaned forward, my nipples grazing his chest. Gently, I kissed his neck, flicking my tongue over it again. His body felt hard beneath mine, pure steel.

He gripped my hair, pulling my ear to his lips. His other hand flexed on my bum, his grip punishing. He whispered in my ear, "I want you as a lover, and I have from the moment I saw you. I want you naked in my bed, always. I want you to be mine."

"There it is." I licked his neck.

He ripped the leaves off my hips, and my breath sped up. I ripped his clothes off him, and we moved to the rhythm of the drum.

* * *

NAKED AND SATIATED, I fell back on the soil. My head felt *slightly* clearer for the moment, but I didn't think that would last long.

I wanted to stay here forever, just Ruadan, the forest, and me. I felt his hands brushing over my skin as he wrapped my body in leaves again. I opened my eyes to watch him work, and I brushed a strand of his blond hair out of his eyes.

Unfortunately, we couldn't stay here forever, and we needed that antidote before we lost our battle completely.

My muscles started to tense. We had a fae mage to bring home, and a psychopath to destroy. And we had just over an hour until that same psychopath unleashed a plague.

With a new set of leaves tied over my chest, I sat up.

"Can you smell her now?" I asked. "Your mage friend."

He turned to look at the bonfire through the trees, and his eyes narrowed. "She's here."

"Good." I pulled on my bug-out bag. "What does she look like? What's her name?"

"Aerwyn. She's short. Amber eyes. Pale, golden skin. Curvy."

We began walking, and the scent of burning cedar curled around me. Something about the description of her bothered me.

"She has purple hair," he added. "With a streak of blue."

I frowned. "So she looks exactly like me, but with a blue streak in her purple hair."

"I wouldn't say that, exactly."

"And you slept with her, right?"

"Slept?"

"You had sex with her."

"It was a long time ago," he said.

I clenched my teeth. It wasn't important. The important thing about my relationship with Ruadan was that he planned to kill me at some point, but he just didn't know it yet.

A hollow opened in my chest, and I breathed in deeply, trying to calm myself.

I stole a quick glance at Ruadan. Could I trust him well enough to tell him the truth? I didn't think so. Ruadan seemed to put duty above everything else.

As we reached the bonfire, a flash of purple hair caught

my eye. Aerwyn was dancing around the fire, swaying her hips seductively, a slow, languid movement. She wore a mask of oak leaves and wildflowers.

I took a deep breath, swaying slightly. "Any tips on how I could convince her to help us? All I know about her is that she hates men."

"Use that."

Not super helpful, but okay.

I felt weird interrupting her dance, but I crossed to her anyway, the bonfire heating my skin. I needed to get her alone, and to do it in a way that wouldn't call too much attention to our conversation. I had to look like an ecstatic reveler.

I tried to sway my hips a little, too, as I sidled up to her. Up close, she didn't look exactly like me—her mouth was a bit smaller. I couldn't see her face completely under the mask, but she looked beautiful.

I grabbed her by the hand. I pulled her away from the fire, and she laughed, skipping along by my side as I led her from the clearing.

Once we'd moved deeper into the forest, I turned to her. She smiled at me, her cheeks pink. Giggling, she grabbed my waist, moving in for a kiss.

I held up a hand to gently stop her. "Okay, that's … you seem very nice, but that's not why I'm here."

"It's not?" She was still smiling. "I like you because you look like me." She had a lilting accent, and I thought her first language might be Fae. She tried to pull me closer again.

"Aerwyn. I need your help," I said.

She cocked her head, her smile disappearing. "How did you know my name?"

"I came here with someone you knew." What was my best angle? "Okay, here's the story. I've been poisoned by Arubian's hounds' claws, and so have my friends, and we

194

heard you could help with that," I blurted. "Can you give us a potion or whatever?"

Behind her mask, I saw her amber eyes widen. "Arubian?"

"Yes."

"Sure. I can make a potion. If you don't get it, the toxins will eat your brain."

My chest tightened. "That sounds pretty bad."

She blinked at me. "I can tell you're telling the truth." She brushed a strand of hair out of my face. "But what did you mean *us*? Who did you come here with? I need the *whole* truth."

I didn't suppose I could just gloss over that bit and get back to the potions. "Umm...."

"Don't lie to me," she snapped. "I always know. And without my help, your brain will become liquid."

My throat had gone dry, but the truth had worked before. "I'm here with Ruadan, Prince of Emain. He's the Grand Master of the Institute we're protecting in London. You don't need to see him, you could just give us the potion. Please."

Fury flashed in her eyes, and she gripped my shoulders so hard I thought she was going to break something. "Ruadan?"

"He mentioned you might have a history...." I trailed off, my head woozy again. Which, I reminded myself, was my brain starting to liquidize. "If we could just get back to the potion."

"He broke my heart. Completely shattered me. He seduced me, made me fall in love with him. He made me depend on him. I *needed* him. And he left me." Her thumbs were digging into me. "He just left. He shattered me completely. He'll do the same to you."

The air around us thinned, breeze growing cold.

"The betrayal will kill you before the sword ever does."

CHAPTER 29

My heart skipped a beat. Had she actually said that last part—those words I so often said to myself? "Wait, what did you just say?"

"I said he shattered me completely."

I shook my head, still catching my breath. "I'm sorry."

"He *likes* breaking hearts," she hissed. "He feeds off it."

My chest hurt. He'd break my heart, too. It was as inevitable as death.

It took me a moment to put together the pieces completely. "He feeds off heartbreak? That's his fomoire drive."

She nodded. "Oh, yeah. Real charming."

That woman who'd been singing karaoke in the pub, mascara streaming down her face—Ruadan had seemed completely fascinated by her. Now, it all made perfect sense. He'd been feeding off her heartbreak.

A tendril of pain coiled through me. Had he said he wanted me in his bed? He'd feed off my pain, too.

Still, Ruadan's dark side was not my top concern right now. We needed the godsdamned antidote. Even with my liquidizing brain and the delirium of Wrenne, I had a ruth-lessly practical side that could take over when I really needed it—the survivor in me that had kept me alive.

I needed the poison out of me. I needed Baleros dead. My survival depended on it.

"I'm sorry about Ruadan," I said. "But I still need your help."

She crossed her arms. "Fine. But I'll need to punch Ruadan in the face."

"That's fine with me."

I took her by the hand again, leading her back to Ruadan, who stood in the shadows of the oak grove. He was holding something in his hand, but I didn't have a chance to see what it was.

As soon as we reached him, Aerwyn pulled her hand away from mine. She ran over to him and punched him hard in the jaw.

He hardly moved, just a sharp turn of his head. He managed to hold onto whatever was in his hand.

"Hi, Aerwyn."

Aerwyn clutched her fist, wincing from the pain. Then, she shoved a finger in Ruadan's face. "You are a bad, bad man." She pushed the mask up on her face and stared at me. Now, I could see we looked a bit different, her lashes and eyebrows lighter than mine. "What's your name?"

"Arianna."

"All right, Arianna. Give me a minute."

She disappeared into the shadows, and I turned to look at Ruadan.

"Is your face okay?" My voice came out sounding angry. I felt like he'd already broken my heart, even if he hadn't. He would, though. Of course he would.

"My face is fine." He held out his hand, and for the first

time, I realized what he was holding. A wreath of leaves, threaded with bluebells. "I thought you might like this."

For just a moment, I forgot all about the fomoire issue, the impending heartbreak, the kill list. "You made me a crown."

"I thought you'd look beautiful wearing that." His voice skimmed over my body. "And nothing else."

Then, I remembered everything Aerwyn had told me, and it all came crashing back into my muddled mind—how he made people love them, then broke their hearts. How he wanted me dead but didn't know it yet. I turned away from him, clutching the wreath. How long until he realized the truth about me, before he put it all together?

When I turned back, fear slammed into me. Ruadan stood before me in his nightmarish form—black, star-flecked wings, dark eyes, a silver sheen on his skin. Fully transformed, dark horns gleamed on his head.

His lip curled, exposing his canines. "Creatures like you don't belong on earth," he snarled.

He was going to rip my heart out of my chest.

I had to kill him first, and my shoulder blades itched. I'd let my death magic wash over him. *Sever all emotional ties. Kill them all.*

I gasped, stumbling back from him, trying to hush the death instinct.

Then, as quickly as the image had arrived, it flitted away again. Ruadan's wings had disappeared, the horns gone.

A hallucination? I held my chest, gasping for breath.

He frowned at me. "Are you all right? You look terrified."

"It's the poison," I stammered. "I need that godsdamned antidote." I exhaled slowly.

Sever all emotional ties. This won't end well.

With a shaking hand, I laid the wreath on the ground.

"That's sweet, but I'm not taking that with me. This won't end well."

Had I said that out loud?

When I looked up at him again—for just a moment—I saw a look of hurt in his eyes. It was gone again, so fast I couldn't be sure it had been real.

Just then, Aerwyn sashayed back through the shrubs holding a fistful of herbs and moss. "I've already blessed them with the power of the Old Gods. Just mash this up with rainwater, boil it, and let it cool. Once you drink it, it will counteract the effects of the poison. Will you be able to get it back safely?"

I nodded. I had Tupperware in my backpack that should keep it secure.

Ruadan looked at her. "Thank you for—"

"Go fuck yourself!" she shouted.

With that, she was off into the shrubs again. I shoved the handful of herbs and moss into my plastic container, then sealed it up tight.

Within moments, the cold waters of the portal were ripping open the ground.

* * *

I HELD a warm cloak around myself in the throne room, watching as Aengus drank the last bit of the antidote. *Less than an hour left.*

I'd already drank mine, and within moments, my head had felt miraculously clear again.

Outside, the sun was dipping lower, growing redder. Real, this time, and not the work of Nyxobas. Any moment, now, we'd be able to make our way to Hampton Court Palace. But first, Ruadan wanted us to secure the Institute.

I strapped a sword and sheath to my waist. I wasn't

exactly sure what the plan was yet, but I felt better when I wore it.

Melusine sidled up beside me. "What was the Wrenne festival like?"

"I'm just glad we missed the prisoner-burning," I muttered. Small mercies.

"What?"

"The burning of the sixteen prisoners at the bonfire."

She frowned. "They don't burn people. It's a fertility festival. The poison must have confused you."

I scowled. Ruadan's weird sense of humor again, I supposed.

Another explosion rocked the Institute, the sound nearly deafening. I clamped my hands over my ears. Who'd given them all the grenades? Bloody hells.

At that moment, Ruadan crossed into the room, weapons crammed under each of his enormous arms.

"We need to contain this, now," he said. "We have to defend the Institute before they rip through the outer wall completely. Wear cowls to hide your identity. Shoot anyone attacking us."

I crossed to Ruadan, pulling a bow out of his arms and a quiver of arrows. I had a sword on me, but it wouldn't do much good from the Tower.

I pulled the quiver over my torso and held onto the wooden bow. It had been my mother's weapon of choice, and she'd taught me to use it for hunting deer. Never for hunting humans, but like I'd said … women could be adaptable.

"Queen Macha and the other knights are already on the battlements," said Ruadan.

I pulled a cowl over my head.

Ruadan rushed out of the hall—already on his way to slaughter the humans attacking us—and I followed close behind him.

I moved swiftly, running through the hall, the corridors, the courtyard under the blood-red sky, until I found my way to the parapet that loomed above the Thames. To my right, half a tower had crumbled to the pavement, dust clouding the air. Scorch marks darkened the stone.

Strangely enough, the idea of killing was a relief from my thoughts. Better to kill some attackers than to think about Ruadan—about that damned wreath, and the look on his face when I'd thrown it on the ground.

I couldn't even be sure that look had been real. I'd been dosed on up hallucinogenic toxins, and the truth was that he was a fomoire who wanted me dead. As I nocked an arrow, the thought hit me like a bullet. Of *course* he fed off heartbreak. The man was an incubus as well as a fomoire. On one side, he fed from love—the other, from love's destruction.

I stared as a man in a tracksuit below us reared back his arm, ready to hurl a grenade. I set my sights on him.

Seriously, *where* the fuck had they got grenades from? Baleros, probably.

I loosed the arrow, and it caught him in the chest. He fell to the ground, and the humans around him screamed. They looked so furious, so enraged, that I wondered for a moment if Baleros had cast some sort of rage spell on them. But no— it was really just that they were terrified of us, and humans acted like sadists when they were scared.

A man in an Arsenal T-shirt gripped a Molotov cocktail. I nocked another arrow and released it. My shot caught him in the neck.

I didn't love killing humans. It seemed just a little too easy, and they were supposed to be our allies.

Maybe I could try another method of crowd control.

I crouched below the parapet and jammed my hand into my bug-out bag. I pulled out another arrow, along with tissues and a tiny plastic bottle of whiskey. I wrapped the tissues around the arrow's tip, then poured the whiskey on it. My gaze flicked to the sky.

Almost time to go.

I snatched my lighter from the bag, then lit the arrow's tip until a flame roared up in the dim light. Then, I aimed it just before the mob, and I let it fly. The humans started to scatter, pushing away from the flaming arrow. A few more fiery arrows, and they were scrambling over themselves to get away.

With the threat of flaming arrows raining down, the humans began to scatter at last.

CHAPTER 30

Thirty minutes left.

I glanced at the sky, which was darkening to a muddy purple over the Thames. As soon as the last of the sun rays fell behind the horizon, it was time to take on Baleros.

We'd never finalized our plan, and I had a bad feeling Ruadan planned to slip off on his own—that he'd be ready to simply give himself up if it didn't work out.

Baleros was always one step ahead, and he'd be ready for Ruadan. No way in hells was I letting the Grand Master play into Baleros's hands. Gripping my bow, I whirled. I needed to find Ruadan before he left, as the last of the orange light dropped behind London's skyline.

Where was he? From here, I could see the other knights on the battlements, and Baleros's flag flew proudly over us all. But everyone had their hoods on, and I couldn't tell which knight was Ruadan. I strained my eyes, trying to search for his dark magic.

I sniffed the air, searching for the scent of pine and apples.

Where was he?

As the sun disappeared, there were just enough shadows to use the lumen stone. It glowed around my neck. I touched the stone, feeling the electric magic crackling through me. I stared at one of the inner walls, leaping to the walkway.

I landed hard on the stone, then peered over the wall, catching my breath. As I looked out over the courtyard, I gasped. Ruadan had already opened a portal in the middle of the grassy courtyard.

Worse, he'd already gone through it.

I swallowed hard as the portal began to close. Before I could waste another heartbeat, I shadow-leapt through the darkness, plunging into the icy waters. The portal closed above me.

* * *

I HELD my breath under the water, feeling my sword weighing me down. Light pierced the surface, cold rays cutting through the darkness. I kicked my legs hard, pushing myself up toward the light.

But something was wrong, and it took me a moment to figure out what it was. Why was there so much light? It was supposed to be night—that was the whole point.

Dread coiled through my chest, tightening my lungs. This wasn't right.

I reached the air, gasping. I had a moment of relief—night still covered the sky, stars gleaming above me. Ruadan had opened a portal right into the Thames itself, and the ruddy bricks of Hampton Court palace loomed over the river.

Although it was still night, the palace itself blazed with an unnatural, golden light.

I treaded water in the chilly Thames, staring up at the palace's grandeur over the grassy bank.

So, *this* was Baleros's plan—light up the palace from the

inside out, use the goddess's fire magic to extinguish all the shadows. There was no way Ruadan could leap through the palace when it was lit up like a Christmas tree.

Where *was* he, though? I kicked in the water, swimming over to the river's edge. Catching my breath, I hoisted myself out onto the damp grass. With the bright light of the palace streaming over me, I felt exposed. Still, I didn't see any jackdaws roaming around, ready to blow me up.

A flicker of darkness caught my eye. Like a caged animal, Ruadan was pacing the riverside. His movements looked feral, and I didn't get the sense he was quite as controlled as he normally was.

Baleros unnerved Ruadan just as he did me. He warped our ability to act logically, to defend ourselves. That ruthlessly pragmatic side—the survivor in us—got lost in the haze of emotions when Baleros was involved.

I crossed to him, shoulders tensed. I had the uneasy feeling that he might turn on me like a wolf about to die. The fact that he didn't even notice me coming showed me how lost he was in his own fury. When I was only a few feet away from him, he turned sharply, his shadows devouring the golden light around him. From the darkness, his pale gaze seared me.

"What are you doing here?" he asked sharply.

I need to get the mist army before you do. "I wanted to make sure you didn't die or turn yourself in."

His magic slashed the air around him, a maelstrom of darkness. "What powers do you have that you could help a demigod? I'm not clear on that."

There was an edge of steel in his voice. A challenge. His dark magic rippled over me.

"We have twenty-five minutes until Baleros unleashes the Plague," Ruadan went on. "If I go into his palace, I'll likely end up dead. If I don't, half the city of London will die." He raked a hand through his hair. "Do you know what it's like when people die of the Plague? Flesh rotting with gangrene, swollen glands that split open and bleed—tokens of death. Lungs that stop working, vomiting blood—"

I clamped my hands over my ears. "I get it. Stop. I get that it's terrible. This isn't helping." My head was spinning. I hadn't been entirely familiar with the symptomology of the Black Death. Why would I have been? But this sounded … uncomfortably familiar. I'd seen this before. And, apparently, so had Ruadan. "How do you know so much about it?"

"It's how my wife died."

"I thought you said—" I nearly said *my father*, but I stopped myself. "I thought you said Adonis killed her."

He shot me a sharp look. "He did. I told you about the legend, and it's true. She died of the Plague—but I could see the dark magic on her. The magic had a certain scent to it, something Angelic."

"What did it smell like?"

"Myrrh."

The word set frost racing up my spine.

Myrrh. The scent of Adonis.

Some legends weren't true. Others were. I schooled my features to calm.

"That's why I think Adonis is working with Baleros," he went on. "He must have escaped his realm. He's not an ordinary angel. He's practically a god. Maybe he opened his world. Maybe he came through the portal after me."

I breathed in deeply. I could have sworn I smelled the scent of myrrh on the air here now.

My throat tightened. "But why would they work together?"

"It would make sense for them to form an alliance, wouldn't it?" He paced over the grass. "They both want me dead. Baleros wants the World Key. Adonis will be hell-bent on vengeance for causing the death of his wife. He'll want to stop me from killing him and his son. It's why the cult we found was worshiping Adonis. Feeding him."

Something cold and dark was cutting at me from within. "And you think only Adonis can cause the Black Plague." I was clinging to shreds of hope. "You don't think it could be a spell?"

"I think Adonis *is* the Plague." The air had chilled to a wintry cold. "The plagues of the fourteenth century, the seventeenth century, the plagues that wiped out half of Europe. That was Adonis losing control of himself—every time. I'm sure of it. When I invaded his world, he created a plague then, too. I saw them die before me. The same symptoms—the buboes, the purpling skin and rotting flesh. That's what I mean when I say he has to die. A creature like him is too dangerous for this world."

All the air had left my lungs. It was hard to argue with this point. I'd seen it happen myself. I remembered what my mum had looked like.

A creature who killed half of Europe just by getting emotional. Of *course* such a monster could no longer stay on Earth.

Ruadan could never know the truth about me. Maybe we'd shared a moment in the sewers, and another in the forest. Maybe he thought he trusted me. But once he found out who I really was, duty would compel him to kill me.

And maybe he wouldn't be wrong. What dark kernels of destruction were blooming in me, even now?

Sharp edges of pain pierced my chest, and I hated the fact that tears were starting to sting my eyes.

Ruadan was staring at me closely, like he'd read my expression but didn't know what to make of it. And worse— was his body *glowing?* The fucker was feeding off my broken heart already.

Anger ignited. I didn't think about it before I swung for his face, before my knuckles connected with his perfect jaw. The sting of bone meeting bone was a satisfying release.

He touched his cheek, staring at me with a shocked expression. Still glowing, the bastard.

"What's going on?" he asked sharply. "That's the second time a woman has punched me tonight."

"Nothing. What's going on is that we have about twenty minutes to get into that palace and try to kill Baleros. Because if we don't, every terrible thing you just described will happen to everyone we know. Melusine, Ciara, Aengus. Every human and everyone at the Institute will have their fingers rot off or whatever. And I'm not letting you give yourself over without a fight. That's it. That's final. We're in this together."

Ruadan stared at me for a long minute, and the breeze rushed over the Thames. "We probably won't come out of there."

"I know."

But a creature like me shouldn't be here in the first place, right?

Ruadan's jaw twitched. "Go back to the Institute. I'll do this alone. I'm the one he wants."

"No. We can work together. You can use your magic to make it dark in there, while I try to find Baleros. Maybe we don't get to capture him and take him through a portal, but at least I can hack him to pieces with an iron sword. I can slow this down, give us a few more days. And if Adonis—" My voice broke. "If Adonis is there, we can slow him down. Everyone can die, even the Horseman of Death. You have those magic stones or whatever, right? The ones that can kill him?"

"I'm ordering you to return." Steel laced his voice.

I'm done taking orders tonight. I turned, heading for the palace. "If you won't bring the darkness, I'll go in the light."

I marched over the grass toward the beaming palace. The faint scent of myrrh curled around me.

Dad?

"Arianna," Ruadan barked. He was moving after me.

I turned to face him. "There's nothing you can do to stop me from running into that palace. I get to choose when I die, not you. I don't care if you're the Grand Master. There's not an army on Earth that could drag me back through that portal right now. We're finding Baleros together. Now, we have less than twenty minutes. I need you to make it dark."

Ruadan's eyes were black as pitch. He turned to the palace. "At the first sign that your life is in danger, I'm giving myself up."

"That's sweet." Ruadan would have no idea why I sounded so bitter. *The fact is, my love, you're gonna be the first one to draw a sword on me when you find out the truth.*

Another hot tear spilled down my cheek, and I hated myself for it.

What I was not expecting was for Ruadan to pull me into his arms at that moment, to envelop me with his warmth in a gentle embrace.

For just a moment, I let myself rest my head against his chest. And for just a moment, I imagined that this was our reality—that we were just a normal couple who loved each other. That we weren't possibly rushing to our deaths, that we weren't keeping secrets from each other. For just that perfect moment, I pretended this wasn't the end. I listened to his heartbeat, and I breathed in the scent of pines and apples.

Then, I pulled away from him again. "I don't know anything about this palace, or any palaces, really. Where would we find Baleros in there?"

Ruadan sniffed the air. "We'll have to scent him out."

"Roses. Sickly sweet roses."

"I remember."

I closed my eyes, breathing deeply to pick through all the smells. After a moment, the faint scent of roses floated on the wind from one of the palace walls—inside one of the courtyards.

"I've got it," I whispered.

"Wait," said Ruadan. He pulled a silver ring off his finger, and his violet magic pulsed and sparked around it until the whole ring glowed with his magic. "This will help you move undetected. My Wraith magic, distilled."

He handed it to me, and I slipped it onto my thumb. His magic skimmed over my skin. There was something strangely intimate about using another person's magic. It was like sleeping in their bed or wearing one of their shirts over your bare skin—a strange closeness to another person's essence, a little spark of their soul.

We walked over the grasses, along the perimeter of Hampton Court Palace, moving closer to the scent of roses coming from the courtyard. We kept at enough of a distance that we weren't bathed in too much light, our forms indistinct with Ruadan's magic.

The silence that bloomed around us had thorns.

I couldn't admit the truth to Ruadan, but I couldn't hide it from myself anymore. The other truth. The part about how I'd fallen in love with him.

For such a complicated thing, it was as simple as that. I didn't have a choice in it, any more than the ocean had a choice about crashing against the shore. It just was.

CHAPTER 31

*H*is fingers brushed against mine as we walked, and an electrical charge passed between us.

"Why did you punch me?" he asked quietly.

"Why does anything happen?" I asked. "Why does the ocean crash against the shore?" There was that image in my mind again.

"Because of the wind and the moon's gravitational—"

"Okay, that was a bad example."

"Sometimes earthquakes, or—"

"I get it." I swallowed hard. In this day and age, it was hard to think of anything without a viable explanation.

"Whatever it was," he said, "it was an amazingly inadequate answer."

"Says the man who answered literally no questions for years."

At the entrance to the courtyard, the scent of roses grew stronger, and I peered around the corner. There was so much light blazing out of the palace windows that I couldn't see anything within them.

Ruadan's wraith magic flickered around us, disguising us.

Golden light blazed over the court—so bright it looked like daylight. Through the archway, I could see a fountain. Dark red liquid flowed from its ornate spigots—either blood or wine, I couldn't tell.

"We have to go in there," I whispered. "Can you make it a little darker?"

The temperature dropped, and darkness swelled around Ruadan, his pale hair whipping in the wind. A frigid power rippled over the landscape, and the bright golden light dulled to a dusky purple.

Now, there were just enough shadows for me to leap into the courtyard, into the darkness beside the fountain. Ruadan followed behind me, touching down on the cobbles in the shadows.

The palace walls towered high above us. From here, I could smell the distinct scent of claret. But over that, Baleros's rosy smell bloomed on the wind. It was coming from an archway on the other side—just to the left, I thought. Now, I had a pretty good idea of where to leap next.

Ruadan was doing that *indistinct* thing, and I couldn't quite see him, but I could feel his power close to me. "Almost there," I whispered.

Just for a moment, I caught his gaze. Not the shadowy eyes of an incubus, but Ruadan's violet eyes—the real Ruadan.

I wanted to tell him that I loved him, but something stopped me. I think it was that pragmatic survivor in me. The survivor knew it would kill me if my confession was met with silence. I might have had only a few more minutes to live, here, and it might be best if I didn't spend them falling apart emotionally.

Golden light lit up some of the windows, and if I wanted to move around rapidly inside the palace, I'd need even more darkness.

A flicker of myrrh on the breeze, and my pulse quickened. I did not want to find my father here. "I don't feel Adonis's presence." My voice broke as I lied. I hated lying, but I wanted it to be the truth.

An ice-cold wind whipped over me.

"How would you know what his presence feels like?" Ruadan asked.

Shit. I shook my head. "I don't know. I just don't feel anything like angel magic."

A lie. It was all around me, pulsing over my skin. The scent of myrrh tinged the wind under the roses.

I had to stop my father. Stop Adonis. Get the mist army.

I had twenty minutes to do it. No, less now.

Ruadan kept staring at me until I gave his arm a little smack. "We don't have time for this. You need to bring the darkness, now. Cover this place completely in shadows. I've got my iron sword. Let's go."

"You've got three minutes before I announce my presence." He closed his eyes. His body seemed to grow, and a wave of pure, dark power washed over me—thrilling and dizzying at the same time, like standing at the edge of a chasm. The effort of creating night seemed to have consumed him completely, and when I stared at him, it was like looking into the void itself. His body was still as marble. Never had he looked more remote.

When I closed my eyes, stars whirled in my mind over a blanket of vibrant purples and midnight blues.

When I opened my eyes again, shadows had blanketed the entire palace. I couldn't even see Ruadan anymore.

"I need you to stay out here," I whispered. "Promise me you'll stay here. Keep it dark."

His only response was a silky stroke of his magic over my skin, and my spine straightened at the touch.

I turned, then shadow-leapt to the archway. I felt around

in front of me, then pushed through a wooden door. An *unlocked* wooden door. For just a moment, I hesitated. Was that a little too convenient? My heart thundered, and I drew my sword as I stepped inside.

I had to act fast. It was dark as the shadow hell in here. I reached out to feel the room around me—the cold stone of a wall, the swoop of a stone banister up a stairwell. I sniffed the air again, tuning into Baleros's scent.

Tracing my fingertips along the cold stone banister, I swooped up the stairs, toward the rose smell. I landed at the top of a stairwell.

Fifteen minutes left.

I touched the lumen stone at my neck, focusing on the room's interior. Pure blackness, shadows thick as velvet. And yet, by the echoing sounds of my footfalls, I had the sense I was in an enormous hall—one with high ceilings. Just a bit more light would have come in useful right now.

I shadow-leapt farther into the hall, and the overpowering scent of roses hit me. I wanted to throw up. I reached out in front of me to feel for Baleros, certain I'd touch the rough wool of his clothes.

Instead, my fingers touched flowers, their petals soft and wilted.

Actual roses.

Fuck, fuck, fuck. That had been the scent we'd followed? A little less darkness would be helpful, but I couldn't communicate that to Ruadan now.

A footfall behind me turned my head, and my heart leapt into my throat. I cut my sword through the darkness, swinging for the sound of the movement. A grunt and a gargle as the blade went through flesh, through bone. I just had no idea who I was fighting. Another creak of the floor, and I pivoted, my blade hacking into someone's neck. Blood sprayed on my skin.

Who was I fighting? Around me, I could hear the sounds of more footsteps, more guards moving.

Either my eyes had begun to adjust to the darkness or Ruadan was letting up on the shadows, because now I could just about make out the contours of the furniture around me.

Unfortunately, I could also make out the glinting of metal on the people surrounding me.

My stomach leapt. Guards crowded this room, closing in on me. I whirled and ducked, fighting off my attackers. I had to shadow-leap away from them.

Gods below. Was Baleros even in here, or had I simply been lured in by the scent of damn flowers?

Ruadan pulled back a bit more of the darkness. Silver light beamed into the room from stained-glass windows high above us, and I got a better view of the fae around me.

Battle fury thrummed through my blood, and I whirled into action. I drove my sword into a guard, plunging it right into his heart. Magic tickled my shoulder-blades, my power threatening to erupt. Adrenaline surged, blood pounding.

I am the blackening of your skin. I am the silence of a closed throat.

I was a maelstrom of fury, blade meeting flesh, over and over; carving, hacking, destroying….

Bow before me.

Until not a single guard remained.

I stood, catching my breath.

I needed to shadow-leap out of here, to keep moving. Except—I wasn't sure where I needed to go.

I sniffed the air again. Roses. Myrrh.

Dad?

They were here, I was sure of it. Baleros and Adonis.

My heart stuttered at the sight of a large, male form in the corner of the room.

"Dad?" I whispered.

I took a step closer, but a shrill singing rooted me in place. The singing of a bean nighe. I clamped my hands over my ears.

A wall of black, pressing down on my mind. This was the third scent in the room. The chalky scent of calcium, human bones—the stench of death and riverbeds. The bean nighe.

I forced my hands away from my ears, gripping my sword. I was ready to kill.

"Arianna." Baleros's voice, familiar as a lover's touch.

He *was* here. My heart stopped. Where *was* he?

Channeling the magic of the lumen-stone, I shadow-leapt to the silhouette I'd seen. But I found no one there—just an empty corner of the room.

As I got ready to leap again, one of the bean nighe shrieked louder. Someone was about to die.

I whirled, searching the contours of the room for Baleros. Where was he? That stupid vase of roses was confusing me.

I tuned into the sound of the bean nighe instead. Then, I shadow-leapt, touching down behind one of them. She screamed, and I silenced her with a blade through her throat. Why had he brought the bean nighe here?

"Arianna," Baleros said again, this time in a singsong voice that melded with the bean nighe's wild song. "Not your real name, is it?"

Something dark and dangerous was stirring inside me. "No," I said.

I leapt again, landing behind a second bean nighe near the center of the hall. I carved through her with the blade.

"I'm Liora."

CHAPTER 32

hree minutes left.

"Angel of death," said Baleros. "If you were as powerful as your father, I might actually be frightened."

"Where is he?" I demanded.

"Who?"

"Adonis. I can smell him."

A dark chuckle from the shadows. "Miss him, did you? Even after what he did to your family?"

The bean nighe's wails grew louder, echoing off the high ceiling. How many of them were there? At last, the screeching erupted into wild shrieks. Death on the horizon, all around us.

Just like it had in the sewers, a wall of darkness slammed into my skull.

The memory claimed my mind, and I stared at my mother's hair, spread out over the soil. My father, Horseman of Death, had killed them all.

Except ... that wasn't what happened....

I fought against the cage of this vision, desperate to break free.

My fingers shook, legs trembled. I wasn't in the palace anymore. Now, I was back home, crouching behind a mulberry bush. Heart thundering, I stared at the fae invaders. My father had told me to run, but I couldn't tear myself away yet. I pulled my cap lower over my head, shielding my eyes. I could hardly breathe. I didn't know how to fight. My father had told me to hide here, not to move. I wasn't sure I could move if I wanted to, not with fear freezing my muscles.

The invaders rode enormous horses, hair flowing behind them. Darkness pulsed around their powerful bodies. They'd come here to kill us all. They were only a few hundred yards away, now.

My father stood in the clearing, his sword drawn. He didn't look scared at all. Why did he seem so calm? Why wasn't he afraid of dying?

From my hiding spot, I caught a glimpse of red hair—my mother taking cover behind an oak across the clearing. She nocked an arrow, then loosed it. With perfect aim, it struck one of the fae invaders. One after another, she let the arrows fly. I'd seen her kill a deer before, but nothing like this, each arrow finding its mark perfectly.

But there were too many invaders, racing closer, swords drawn.

My father turned to me, spotting me. He shouted at me to run.

They were going to kill us all.

Shimmering midnight wings sprouted from my father's back, each shot through with silver.

My world tilted.

I'd never seen the wings before, and their otherworldly beauty almost shocked me out of the horror of what was happening, almost robbed me of the realization that my father was an angel of death.

That's why they'd come for us—to rid the earth of angels.

The invaders were upon us, now, blades gleaming in the sunlight. My shoulder blades tingled, a dark power threatening to unleash itself. Shadows clouded my mind. I closed my eyes.

This time, I remembered it all—the dark truth I'd been running from for years.

From deep within me, a hurricane of dark magic ripped through the forest, our home. This time, I felt it come from me, wilting the plants around me, stealing breath.

I'm the toxins in your blood, the red drop on your lips. I make your fingers curl, black as mold. I'm a mother eating her young, the skull in the soil. All fall before me.

Dark magic erupted from my ribs, from my gut, a maelstrom of death—suffocating, poisoning all life around me.

I opened my eyes again.

All the fae around us were falling to the earth like autumn leaves. Blood dripped from my mother's mouth onto the soil. Her skin had turned purple, fingers blackening….

It had been me. The plague.

I ran from the clearing. Death sang its dirge around me as I sprinted, crunching over the soil.

I am the stalker that creeps up behind you. I will steal your food and your breath.

I ran until my legs were ready to give way, until I my lungs ached for air. I ran until I found the glimmering, star-flecked portal.

* * *

MY OWN SCREAMS rang in my ears as I snapped free from the memory. I wanted blood.

I am the stalker that creeps up behind you. I will steal your food and your breath.

At last, I understood.

My father hadn't killed everyone that day. It had been me. A sharp hollowness pierced me from the inside out. I'd killed my mother. I was as powerful as Adonis, and my magic had slaughtered the whole village.

Had my father been able to bring her back? I had to—

I blinked, looking around. The survivor in me needed me to focus on the present. *Take stock of your surroundings. Stay in the moment. Don't let Baleros distract you.*

I caught my breath, surveying the dark hall around me. Silver light streamed in from the stained-glass windows, washing over the tapestries and the piles of guards I'd killed. Moonlight bathed the roses wilting on all the banquet tables and silvered the two dead bean nighe bleeding on the wood floor.

Adonis wasn't in here. No one living was in here.

While I'd been reliving the worst day of my life, Baleros had slipped away, leaving me distracted.

I wasn't his target. Ruadan was the real target.

A deep voice boomed from outside. "I am Ruadan, Prince of Emain, son of Queen Macha."

My toes curled. *You idiot.*

He was giving up, trying to turn himself in.

With a ragged breath, I gripped my sword, racing down the stone steps.

When I flung open the door to the courtyard, I found Ruadan surrounded by Baleros's entire army—the mist soldiers, the jackdaws in their cloaks. Distantly, I heard the sound of someone chanting an Angelic spell.

My father was an expert in Angelic.

I sniffed the air. Roses—and myrrh.

Fog curled around the darkened courtyard. In the center of the mist army, shadows pooled around Ruadan. He was creating darkness—for me, so I could get away. I wasn't leaving him.

Tendrils of magic snaked through the air around him. His power seemed to be weakening, the star-flecked shimmer of his magic dulling. Why?

The sound of Angelic grew louder. With a jolt of horror, I understood what was happening. Ruadan had said one of the only ways to kill him was to use an Angelic spell—and Baleros, it seemed, knew the exact spell. Baleros was trying to make him mortal.

Panic punched me in the gut.

I sniffed the air, homing in on the roses until I found him. There. Baleros stood all the way on the other side of the courtyard—in the archway, holding a sword. He held something else, as well. Something that gleamed in the moonlight.

A lumen stone glowed around his neck. I couldn't give him the chance to leap away by letting him know I was coming.

I touched my lumen stone, then leapt into the air just before him. Fast as a hummingbird's breath, I swung the sword for his neck as I landed.

A precise arc, a hair's breadth away from his skin. I cut the lumen stone off him, and it fell to the brick.

He stared at me, the corner of his lip twitching. He was gripping a sword, but he couldn't move it. Not with me threatening to slice his jugular.

I steal your food and your breath, draw your ribs out from under your skin....

I pointed my sword at his throat. "Hi, Baleros."

He didn't look concerned. "Tick tock, Liora. I gave you a time limit. Three minutes till nine. I'll need the iron on Ruadan when he gives himself up. I'm sure you understand."

"Where is Adonis?" I asked through gritted teeth. The air smelled heavy with the scent of myrrh.

"I think he'll be disappointed with you."

With a jolt of horror, I realized that the rhythmic

cadences of Angelic were still floating through the air, the spell carrying on where Baleros had left off. Dozens of voices chanted in unison. With the tip of my sword trained on Baleros's throat, I stole a quick look behind me. The jackdaws had simply picked up where Baleros had left off. They all knew the spell. They were going to kill Ruadan right here.

"Stop them," I said.

With a movement so fast I could hardly track it, he brought his sword to my neck. That look I'd stolen had cost me.

Gods*damn* it. I should have just killed him instead of asking about Adonis.

I stared into his eyes, which were lightly crinkled at the corners. The death angel in me longed for release, and my father's magic surrounded us. Where *was* he?

My heart boomed against my ribs, heavy footfalls of a dark beast.

I am the stalker that creeps up behind you when you're trying to find the right words.

A vision flashed in my mind—Ruadan threading flowers together for me.

I couldn't stand here while they killed Ruadan. I had to stop this.

I'm here when you're searching to fill the silence, fleeing the dark truth.

A voice in my mind. A thousand voices, mingling together, high and low, dissonant. Magic raced down my back, my shoulder blades blazing with power. The wind whipped around me, cold and unforgiving.

You hold up a landscape you painted; you grin at your gold; you buy a house on the hill overlooking the lake. You smile proudly. See this? you think. It will last forever. You don't see me looming behind you. I'm a long twilight shadow over cemetery grass. I enshroud your body from the toes up.

Dark ecstasy claimed my mind as wings erupted from my back. I lifted off the earth.

Sweet release, an embrace of the dark truth.

My midnight wings—streaked with gold—lifted me into the air, night wind racing over my skin, tearing at my hair.

I read the shock on Baleros's face.

Bow before me.

From above, I drove my sword into him, impaling him from the skull down, splitting him in two. For just a moment, blood poured out of him. Then, his body erupted into flames, the hot blast knocking me back.

His sword fell to the ground with a clang. And something else, too—a gleaming chalice.

What *was* that? The cup called to me with its own dark magic, and I yearned to pick it up. But it wasn't the time, and I needed to stay in the air. Baleros wasn't truly dead. The Fire Goddess would revive him. But I had his mist army, now, and it was time to deploy them.

My powerful wings lifted me higher over the crowd of jackdaws, and they still chanted.

I raised my sword, shouting my first command to my mist soldiers: "Attack the humans!"

A smiled curled my lips, relief washing over me. Fog curled into the air as the mist soldiers whirled into action. Their swords began carving into the black cloaks.

All fall before me.

From the air, I glanced at Ruadan. My mist soldiers were attacking the jackdaws, but his power was fading fast, coils of star-flecked magic flitting away from his body like smoke on the wind. His eyes were closed, his body hunched as they turned him mortal. The sight of it bruised my heart.

I rob your memories, leave you with only a final glimmer of knowledge. I take that, too. I steal your food and your breath, draw your ribs out under your skin, carve your belly.

I shouted his name, but he couldn't hear me. It was like he was totally collapsing into himself—a black hole of magic. Shadows swallowed him.

The mist army was fighting the humans, but not fast enough. The jackdaws had no fear, and they weren't running. They were standing their ground, chanting. Stealing his immortality.

I'm the green smear on your mouth, the sallow in your skin, the swaying darkness under your feet and your last rasping breath. I'm the eternal darkness that awaits you at the end, and I have always been with you.

Death rippled out of my body like an atomic blast. Euphoria claimed my mind.

From the sky, I stared down at the courtyard to see the humans falling to the ground. Ruadan, too, had doubled over, his enormous form collapsing onto the stone.

In the end, you will all bow before me; you will all lay down your lives and worship at my altar.

Their bodies were a beautiful canvas of purple, red, and black, painted with my brush. My own landscape. Death was my creation.

Ecstasy lit me up as I completed the task I'd been born for. I'd killed them all. They rotted below, bleeding from the mouths, the streaks of red. The Plague was a beautiful mixture of cold hues and warm, purple skin—

The Plague.

The scent of myrrh was overpowering. It was Adonis's scent, but mine, too.

Baleros was winning. Nine o'clock. I was spreading the Plague myself, and the wave of death I'd unleashed was still rippling over the city. My heart was ready to explode. I should be thinking about all of them, about the city of London itself, but only one thought crystallized in my mind.

Was Ruadan still immortal, or had I killed him?

My wings pounded the air like a heartbeat as I swooped to hover over where he lay on the stone.

When I met Ruadan's violet eyes, relief flooded me. But only for a moment. The truth was out now, and he was staring at me in my real form.

With what looked like great effort, he forced himself to stand. Wrath etched his features, and something cold split me in two.

Here I am, Ruadan. A creature never meant to walk the earth. The monster who spreads the Plague.

From the air, I looked out over the horizon, at the midnight magic rippling toward London. I needed to stop the death from spreading. *Could* I stop it?

When I closed my eyes, I saw her again—my mother. This time she looked alive, her body blazing with light. I didn't come from Adonis alone—I'd come from my mother, Ruby, too, a being of light. I could remember her light touch on my skin, the gold in her eyes, her kisses on my cheek when she thought I was asleep.

The waves of death seeped back into me, drawn back from the horizon. I pulled my magic back into myself.

My enormous wings beat the air, and I lowered myself to the ground to face Ruadan—my lover and my enemy.

For the first time since I'd met him, I found him shifted completely. Black leather wings spread out behind him, his eyes swirling with darkness. Two dark horns gleamed on his head. He looked like my nightmarish hallucination—the one where I'd envisioned him trying to kill me.

He was holding something aloft—the gleaming chalice. Dark magic wafted off it. It smelled of myrrh….

The sight of him fully shifted sent ice streaming through my veins and left me breathless. A low growl trembled over my skin, then deepened and rumbled through my gut. The incubus in him had come out completely, and he

225

wanted blood. Violet magic crackled over his muscled body.

Ruadan as an incubus was a strangely beautiful nightmare. Part of my brain was screaming at me to run. But his magic was skimming over my body, and the other half of my brain wanted to take a step closer to him, to bask in his eerie beauty, feel his breath on my neck. Ruadan was dangerous as hells—a hunter who could lure you to your own death.

His body glowed as he fed off my pain.

My finger twitched at the hilt of my sword. Everyone had to die sometime.

CHAPTER 33

*T*he mist army spread out behind me, awaiting my next order. Tendrils of fog curled off their bodies, twining in the river's breeze.

Another flash of the death instinct rattled along my bones, spurring me on to kill the enemy before me. My wings thumped the air, feet lifting off the ground just a little. Maybe … just maybe, if my magic was powerful enough, I could kill even a demigod—Angelic spell or not.

Death, the conqueror, reigns supreme. All fall before me.

My fists tightened, nails piercing my palms. *Rein it in, Liora. Stay in control.*

In the end, all bow to me—even the gods.

The look he was giving me was glacial, eyes black, body unmoving. I gripped my sword as I landed before him. His wings spread out behind him. Long, black claws had grown from his fingertips, and I stared at the unyielding, other-worldly face of a predator.

Gripping the chalice, he stared at Death—his ancient enemy.

Kneel, demigod, or I'll rip the life from your body.

I gritted my teeth, my mind flashing with the image of a wreath made of wildflowers and leaves, the one I'd left in Emain. Emptiness ate at my chest. Half of me wanted to sneak off into the shadows, to curl up like an animal crawling off to die. The other half—the survivor in me—wanted to destroy, wanted to leave this man bleeding on the stone before me.

His cold, lethal stare cut me to the quick.

I'd known that the betrayal would kill me before the sword ever did, and at that moment … the way Ruadan was looking at me, it felt like a battle I was losing.

I felt my wings fold and shrink into my shoulder blades as the death instinct flitted away on the wind.

I tried to read Ruadan's expression, but I found nothing there. Just the icy stare of a void demon. I knew how he moved. If he wanted to, he could rip my heart out before I had the chance to see the first twitch of his muscles.

This painful, jagged silence broke my heart. My chest felt like it was being cleaved in two, and Ruadan's body glowed as he fed from my heartbreak.

I glanced at the chalice he was holding, breathed in the scent of my father. Only then did I understand—distilled magic. My father had never been here at all.

I wasn't the Angel of Death anymore. I wasn't Arianna. I was just Liora, and I'd never felt so alone in my life.

Ruadan's power strengthened as he fed off my pain.

"Adonis didn't have a son," I said. "He had a daughter who dressed like a boy. That was me." I tightened my grip on the sword. "My name is Liora. Half fae, half death angel. I saw your kill list. I'm on it."

Silence pressed down on us, interrupted only by the sound of the wind rushing over the river.

I didn't see Ruadan move—just a dark sweep of wind, then I felt his body behind me, his warmth pressing against me. He traced a clawed fingertip over my collarbone, and something dangerous and electrical raced through my blood. It felt like a caress, one tinged with sharpness. It was a warning, too. My head would be gone before I had a chance to react.

My heart beat so hard I was sure Ruadan could hear it.

"Did he send you?" asked Ruadan.

I could hardly think straight, confusion clouding my mind. "Who? Baleros?" We'd been over this. I already told him the truth.

"Adonis."

Anger roiled. "I haven't seen him since the day you came to kill us. He's not working with Baleros. He never was. That chalice you're holding there is my father's magic distilled. Just like you distilled yours in the ring I'm wearing."

"The Unholy Grail," said Ruadan, his voice pure ice. "Some legends are true. It's a magic that doesn't belong on Earth. The destroyer of worlds."

"Speaking of not belonging, you should never have come for us." Rage laced my voice, an anger I didn't know I'd been sheltering. If Ruadan hadn't invaded that day, I wouldn't be here. "You didn't belong in our world. We were fine until you came."

I stole a glance behind me, at his powerful body looming over me. In the V of his dark shirt, the World Key glowed with gold. Those few inches of skin were the root of all this chaos. Anger snapped through my nerve endings, ready to explode.

"From where I'm standing, you're the destroyer of worlds." The fury in my voice surprised even me. "We weren't hurting anyone where we were. We were locked in our own world. You crushed it." I elbowed him hard in the chest, but he hardly moved. "What do you expect when you invade a place? You think you can come to kill people and they won't fight back? Guess what, Ruadan? It wasn't my father who killed everyone. It was me. I killed your cohort. I killed your brothers. I killed my mum, too. That was me. I didn't know it until the bean nighe made me relive it just now. I'm powerful, just like my father. Now you know. I'm on your list. So what are you going to do?"

I stole another look behind me. Darkness swathed him, mist and shadows curling around him in wild whorls. Silence cloaked the courtyard, coldness danced up my spine. Any moment now, he'd rip my head off like I'd seen him do to his enemies.

The tip of his claw traced over my neck. This wasn't Ruadan—this was the incubus.

Or was it the same thing? I told myself that the Angel of Death wasn't me. I told myself I was just Liora, and that was all there was to it. But maybe we couldn't carve ourselves up that way, into neat little parts. Death was a part of me—just like this cold, predatory demon was a part of Ruadan. We all had our own ways of protecting ourselves. This was Ruadan's.

I reached up, and I ran my fingertips along the inside of his wrist, the vulnerable part. Then, I kissed his skin.

His arm stiffened. Then, an almost inaudible exhale—a hint of relief.

At last, he spoke. "I need the mist army to defend the Institute." His voice was like dark velvet skimming over my body, so smooth I nearly forgot the threat he was delivering.

"There's only one way to get it." It was a dangerous dare, but I needed to see what he would do. My heart slammed against my ribs. I could still do it. If I needed to, I could let the death angel come out.

I pulled his arm from me and stepped away over the cobbles, and he didn't stop me. I turned to face him. Those dark, otherworldly wings still swooped behind him.

He took a step closer to me, and my heart nearly stopped. Then, he simply walked past me, stalking off into the shadows by the Thames.

Emptiness cut me open. In this world, Ruadan and Baleros were the only ones who knew the truth about me, and both reviled me.

A hot tear spilled down my cheek, and I wiped it away. "I can still help you," I called out. "I'll help you defend the Institute."

No response. Only the dark, heavy quiet of the river.

CHAPTER 34

Mist curled around my new room, fogging up the window. I swiped my palm over the cold pane. From here, I had a distant view of the Institute, and the mist army patrolling it—*my* mist army, as I was quickly coming to think of them.

For the past two days, my mist soldiers' eerie presence had been enough to deter the human terrorists from trying to mob the Tower. And while the mist soldiers had helped defend it, the Tower's mages had rebuilt the golden moat.

I had no idea what Ruadan had done with the Unholy Grail, or what he planned to do with it. We hadn't spoken in days.

As I stared out the window, Ciara sidled up to me, crossing her arms. "Aren't you feeling a bit cooped up in here?" she asked. "You haven't left in two days."

I hadn't wanted to take my eyes off the Institute. It had been my home. Maybe I was no longer a Shadow Fae, but I couldn't stop thinking about it.

"I'm fine," I said. "Just keeping an eye on things. What did you hear when you went out today? Did our ruse work?"

"*Our* ruse?" she said. A not-so-subtle reminder that I was no longer a knight. "You mean the Shadow Fae plan to pin the blame on Baleros? *The Sun* already published an article about Baleros, right after a story about two soap stars who were falling out of their bikinis. They're calling Baleros the Trenchcoat Terrorist."

I smiled. "Good. Perfect."

"Things seem to have calmed down a bit since you killed all the jackdaws," she added.

"Any sign of Baleros out there?" I asked.

"I haven't heard anything. Don't you have your mist soldiers looking for him?"

I loosed a long sigh, turning back into the center of the room. Three of the mist soldiers sat on the floor, staring into space. They were here to protect us and occasionally buy snacks. The rest I'd sent out on missions—hunting for Baleros, protecting the Institute. Only, it was hard to get information from them, seeing as they didn't speak. I'd simply sent them out with the instructions to find a man who smelled of roses and wore the mark of Emerazel on his shoulder.

"They haven't turned anything up yet. One of them came back with a handful of roses, and I thought maybe he was trying to give me a message about having found Baleros, but after a while, it became clear that he'd been confused about the mission and thought I wanted roses."

"Well, I need some air," said Ciara. "I'm going out for Kit-Kats."

"At this hour? Just send one of the mist guys."

She shook her head. "I can't sleep if I don't move around some. Anyway, you don't need to worry about me anymore, on account of me being a fire demon."

"Fine. But take a mist guy with you."

"Whatever."

One of the soldiers rose from the floor, fog billowing around him. He followed Ciara out the door.

I stared at the other two, now, wishing they could speak. I didn't like the silence anymore. It felt like I'd been buried alive.

I had hardly anything in the room to distract me. It was a step up from living under a car, like Ciara had, but it was basically an empty apartment. A bare, unheated living room with woodchip walls and an empty fireplace. An adjoining kitchen with a broken washer-dryer and a fridge that didn't work. No furniture.

I hadn't spoken to Ruadan in days. I wasn't a knight anymore, apparently, but he hadn't tried to kill me. Had my mist soldiers gotten me off the kill list? Or had they moved me up it, since Ruadan wanted to control them?

I had no idea what my current status was. Right now, I was in limbo.

I stared out the window at the Institute again. This was beginning to feel a bit sad, frankly—my life on the outside, still obsessed with the palace.

A pile of pillows and blankets lay in a corner of the room, and I crossed to them. I lay down, pulling one of the wool blankets on top of me. In this limbo world of mine, distinctions between daytime clothing and pajamas had no meaning. I just slept in the jeans and T-shirt I was already wearing.

I frowned at the mist soldiers. "Can you guard outside the door? I can't sleep with you staring at me there."

Once they left the room, I pulled off my bra and lay down on the blankets. I lay flat on my back, arms over my head, and I closed my eyes. As I drifted off, I thought of Ruadan's fingertip stroking along my collarbone, sending an electric thrill pounding through my blood. I imagined his skin, the faint taste of salt on his neck. I licked my lips and reached under my T-shirt. My hands brushed over my hardening nipples.

My skin heated, and my eyes opened. And when they did, my heart started to gallop out of my chest.

Ruadan was there—standing above me, his pale violet eyes piercing the darkness. I pulled my hands out from under my shirt.

"Are you here to kill me?" I asked breathlessly.

"No."

Good. Because I wouldn't want to have to unleash my dark side again. "Were you watching me while I slept?" I snapped. "Creep."

"I'm half-incubus. Creepily looming over people while they sleep is part of my nature."

"Have you come to ask me back to the Institute?"

He shook his head, and my heart sank. "No."

"Then why are you here?" That rage erupted in my tone again. I couldn't help how I'd been born.

"The Unholy Grail. The Plague, contained in a chalice. It's the ultimate bargaining chip."

"Okay. And?"

"Its existence is a threat to every living creature on Earth. But only one person can destroy it. The person who made it."

I shook my head. "My father. Why would he have made a chalice like that?"

"I guess we'll find out."

Warmth flickered between my ribs. Was I going home? "So, you don't want to kill him anymore."

"Destroying the Unholy Grail is our priority."

Cold. Clinical. An icy demon of the void.

"You want to open the world again. The portal to my home," I said quietly.

My chest tightened. What would we find there? My

father, alone? Left with no one but the people I'd killed all those years ago? Nothing but the bodies surrounding him?

My father, the fallen angel, left in a world on his own, surrounded by death. I shouldn't have left him there.

I moved for Ruadan, so fast I didn't know what I was doing. I gripped his forearms, fingernails digging into his flesh. "You have to take me to him, Ruadan." It was the voice of my death angel, the voice of many.

His calm, soothing magic whispered over me. "I need to be able to trust you."

"And I need to trust you."

No reply. Classic Ruadan.

He plucked my hands off his arms. Then, with a furrow between his eyebrows, he reached into his cloak. He pulled out a wreath—one made of oak leaves and threaded with honeysuckle.

He handed it to me.

Shocked, I took it from him. "What does this mean?" I asked.

He looked as confused as I was. I wasn't sure I'd ever seen him look confused before. "I don't know."

He rose, heading for the door.

"Tomorrow, we find Adonis."

The door closed behind him.

I turned to watch out the window until I saw the blur of dark wind through the night—Ruadan heading back to the Institute.

The Grand Master might not like it, but he needed me. He needed my mist army. He needed me to speak to Adonis.

I lifted the wreath to my head.

* * *

THANK you for reading Court of Darkness. One more book —Court of Dreams—will follow in this series.

This book is part of the *Demons of Fire and Night* world.

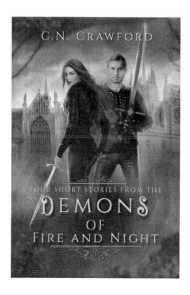

JOIN US ON FACEBOOK!

ACKNOWLEDGMENTS

Thanks to my supportive family, and to Michael Omer for his fantastic feedback and help managing my many author crises. Thanks to Nick for his insight and help crafting the book.

Robin Marcus and Isabella Jack Pickering are my fabulous editors. Thanks to my advanced reader team for their help, and to C.N. Crawford's Coven on Facebook!

ALSO BY CRAWFORD C.N.

For a full list of our books, check out our website.

https://www.cncrawford.com/books/

And a possible reading order.

https://www.cncrawford.com/faq/

Made in United States
North Haven, CT
27 March 2023

34617234R00148